From the Nancy Drew Files

ASSIGNMENT: Act as government courier to deliver a document vital to top-secret negotiations with a country on the brink of revolution.

CONTACT: Senator Marilyn Kilpatrick—*capable and dedicated. But can she keep the unstable country of San Carlos from going completely over the edge?*

SUSPECTS: Teresa Montenegro—*world-class tennis champion from San Carlos and Nancy's picture-perfect double. She may know more than she's telling about her country's murderous affairs.*

Roberto—*Teresa's darkly handsome coach and boyfriend. He's supposed to be fighting the dictator of San Carlos. But whose side is he really on?*

Señora Adelita Ramirez—*Teresa's chaperon. Is she protecting Teresa or is she keeping an eye on her for a corrupt government?*

COMPLICATIONS: Nancy is mistakenly abducted by terrorists. Then Teresa is tricked into a secret rendezvous just when she's scheduled for a match. Nancy agrees to double for her on the court. Will she fool the thousands of spectators? And can she outwit the sniper in the stands?

I0433508

Other Nancy Drew Files™ available in Armada

THE NANCY DREW FILES™

Case 7
Deady Doubles

Carolyn Keene

ARMADA

First published in the USA in 1987 by
Simon & Schuster Inc.
First published in Great Britain
in Armada in 1988

Armada is an imprint of
the Children's Division, part of
the Collins Publishing Group,
8 Grafton Street, London W1X 3LA

Nancy Drew and *The Nancy Drew Files*
are registered trademarks of
Simon & Schuster Inc.

Printed and bound in Great Britain by
William Collins Sons & Co. Ltd, Glasgow

Deadly Doubles

Chapter

One

WHEN IS THAT phone going to ring?" Nancy Drew stalked out of her bedroom and across the hotel suite's living room. She paused in the doorway of the bedroom on the far side, where her two best friends were unpacking.

"It's twenty minutes to two right now," George Fayne said, groaning. She glanced from her watch to her cousin, Bess Marvin, who was sharing the room with her. "If that woman doesn't phone in the next two minutes, we're going to miss the opening tennis match!"

It was a hot summer afternoon. Half an hour earlier, Bess, George, and Nancy had checked into the two-bedroom suite at the Alexandria,

Virginia, hotel. George, an avid athlete, had recently been concentrating on her tennis game, and at her urging the other two had come with her to watch the International Women's Semi-Pro Tennis Tournament. It was being held at Loudon College, not far from Washington, D.C.

"Senator Kilpatrick did phone at one, as she promised," Nancy said. "The desk clerk gave me the message. It wasn't her fault we got caught in all the airport traffic!" Marilyn Kilpatrick was an old law-school friend of Nancy's father. When she had heard from him that Nancy and her friends were going to be in Alexandria, she had asked Nancy to run an errand for her, and Nancy had felt that she couldn't very well say no. "If she said she'll call back and asked me to wait, she'll call," Nancy added.

"Traffic jams wouldn't have *been* a problem if we'd flown down yesterday the way we planned," George pointed out. "Instead of going to that meet-the-players party last night, we were still in River Heights, waiting for your top-secret phone call from the senator." She pulled off the khaki shirt she'd worn for traveling and tossed it onto her bed. "You know something? I'm beginning to have a lot more sympathy for Ned Nickerson."

"Sympathy for Ned?" Nancy exclaimed,

frowning. "Why?" Then her brow cleared. "Oh, you mean because he wasn't able to come to the tournament with us."

"No, she means because even Ned can't be sure that a mystery won't mess up plans you've made," Bess put in, only half laughing.

"Right!" George began rummaging in her suitcase for a tennis crewneck. "I'm sure it's great for Ned to be famous detective Nancy Drew's numero uno guy, but never knowing when a mystery's going to spoil a romantic moment must drive him crazy!"

Nancy's blue eyes twinkled. "Ned manages! And look who's talking about making boyfriends feel insecure!" Bess—small, blond, and curvy—was famous for the speed with which she collected—and then dropped—good-looking boys.

"Ned knows he's my main man in any language," Nancy went on more seriously. "But why do I have to keep telling you that Senator Kilpatrick's errand has nothing to do with a case?"

"Is that why you've been carefully avoiding telling us what it *is* about?" George asked bluntly.

Nancy reddened. All at once, Senator Kilpatrick's warning rang in her ears. *"Tell no one,"* the senator had said. Despite the muggy summer heat, Nancy felt a chill.

3

Bess gave her an odd look but changed the subject deftly. "That 'numero uno' bit means George is brushing up on her Spanish in case she meets that Central American tennis star the TV reporters are making such a fuss about."

"Teresa Montenegro isn't Central American, she's from San Carlos," George corrected her. "That's in *South* America. And she's not a star—not yet. Nobody outside of San Carlos has had a chance to see her play till now. But she's supposed to be really great. I can't wait to watch her!"

"If we ever get there, you mean." Bess began to wriggle into a lavender knit miniskirt. Then she giggled. "Ten to one Nancy's mystery interferes."

"Come off it, you two," Nancy protested, managing a laugh. "I'm meeting somebody to pick up something for the senator, and *that's all!*"

"Su-u-u-re," George drawled. "The lady's only got an office and a staff in D.C., right across the river from here. But she absolutely had to talk to Nancy Drew last night, and she's positively got to have Nancy and nobody but Nancy run this errand. And there's no mystery involved? Who're you trying to kid?"

"This is a simple job—quick and easy. And *no mystery!*" Nancy shook her head vigorously, hoping her red-gold hair hid her blush as she remembered Senator Kilpatrick's words on the phone last night: "Find a way to get into the locker rooms, but don't let anyone find out what you're doing."

"The real mystery," Nancy continued, "is why Bess Marvin, who's allergic to exercise, is in such a hurry to see a tennis tournament."

"If it were a men's tournament we'd understand," George agreed. She looked at her cousin, who was knotting a bright print shirt at her midriff. "I suppose you think that's a tennis outfit," she added, rolling her eyes.

"You're here to watch the tournament and pick up tennis pointers. I'm here to watch the tournament-watchers," Bess said, unruffled. "If you must know, I'm looking for a better grade of boyfriend. One with something in the brains department!"

Nancy's eyes met George's with shared amusement. Bess's most recent great loves had been a rock musician and a skier. Falling for a brain would be a nice change.

"You two take a cab out to the tournament," Nancy said generously. "It'll be my treat. I'll drive the rental car out and meet you just as soon as Senator Kilpatrick has called. That way you won't miss anything."

"Really? Great!" Bess dashed out of the bedroom, taking a brief look in the mirror as she passed it. "If I gain one more pound I won't be able to get into this skirt again," she said mournfully.

"Worry about that later," George said. "I want to get out there and see Teresa Montenegro. See you later, Nancy, okay?"

"Sure," Nancy answered absently as the two girls left. The mention of Teresa Montenegro, the San Carlos player, had made last night's conversation, and her own secret mission, flash vividly back into her head.

Secret mission? What made me think that? Nancy wondered, startled. Her friends were right. She did have mysteries on the brain.

Nancy crossed the suite and went into her bedroom. She stared at her reflection in the bureau mirror, only half seeing it.

The small travel clock she'd set beside the bed ticked loudly. Two o'clock. A quarter after. Half past. When the phone on the bedside table finally rang, Nancy leaped for it so quickly that the little clock went crashing to the floor.

"Senator Kilpat—"

A woman's voice interrupted evenly. "Miss Nancy Drew? This is Senator Kilpatrick's office calling. The senator has asked me to tell you the meet has been postponed until nine o'clock this evening. Same instructions as before. You are to contact the senator immediately afterward and report what happened. Thank you."

The phone went dead.

Not a meeting, *the meet*. That was government talk. Secret Service or CIA talk.

As Nancy changed clothes rapidly, her mind reviewed the instructions Senator Kilpatrick had given her.

"Pick up your special pass at the hotel desk—I sent it over by messenger. It's a government pass, and it should get you through security and into the women's locker room. If the guards give you a hard time, have them call my office. But it would be better if you could get in there without anyone noticing. Your father says you have a blue denim miniskirt. I imagine you have a plain white T-shirt, don't you? . . . Wear that, and do you have some kind of distinctive belt you can wear? . . . A bright red one? Yes, that would be good. I'll see that the courier is notified that that will be your identifying mark. After you receive the information packet, go back to your assigned box seat and stay with your friends for the rest of the match. As soon as you get back to your hotel, call my office and insist on speaking directly to me. I'll alert my staff to connect us at once." That's what the senator had said.

Well, there was no need for the special outfit till that night, so Nancy thrust it into a small duffel bag that she used as a purse and changed into shorts and a knit top in tennis white with a pale blue stripe. Then she ran out of the suite and toward the elevator. If she was lucky, she could just miss the commuter traffic that would soon clog the highways.

The elevator took Nancy directly to the basement-level parking garage. Soon she was out of Alexandria and heading west toward the rolling Virginia countryside. She came to the great shopping mall at Tyson's Corner. Loudon College was only a few miles farther. And didn't the brochure say there's a service road to the college somewhere? Nancy thought. The road to her right had to be it—a wide dirt lane beneath a stand of towering catalpa trees.

Soon Nancy was entering the college grounds. The parking lots near the stadium were filled, but she finally found a space near the dirt lane. She locked the car carefully and threaded her way through the acres of parked cars toward the grandstands.

The sun was high in the sky, and a faint breeze stirred the heavy air. Nancy glanced at her watch. She was pleased to realize that she'd probably missed only part of one match.

She flashed her pass at a guard and asked for directions. Then, as she turned the corner around the first of the gray stone college buildings, she paused. The stadium was across a road and to the left, but maybe there was a shortcut through the building so she wouldn't have to take time to circle the two beyond. Yes, Nancy could see another set of glass doors on the opposite side of the ground floor. She pushed open the door nearest her and started into the cool dimness.

"Señorita, this area is players only." A dark, good-looking, wiry young man wearing tennis clothes caught her arm. But as Nancy spun around, startled, he let go quickly. "Oh, I'm sorry—"

"I'm the one who should be sorry. I didn't know this was off-limits." Nancy smiled. "What's the best way to get to the courts?"

For a moment the athlete just stood and looked at Nancy blankly. Then he shrugged. "Oh, go ahead. Cut through here and you'll get there faster. Just don't tell anyone I said you could do it. Right?"

"Right." Nancy smiled again and pushed through the other set of doors.

As the doors banged shut behind her, hands closed roughly on her shoulders.

For a split second Nancy thought it was the young athlete playing a trick on her. Then she knew, with horror, that it was no trick. She twisted around, trying to get a look at her attacker. The man thrusting a gag into her mouth was middle-aged. He wore a dark, foreign-looking business suit. So did the other two men who held her tightly.

It all seemed to be happening in slow motion.

This isn't real, Nancy told herself dazedly. But it *was* real. She was being kidnapped. And the method was fast, efficient, and effective.

Nancy struggled frantically as she was pulled into the bushes and her hands and feet were bound with ropes. She was thrown like a bundle over a brawny shoulder, and a concealing blanket was tossed over her.

Nancy knew struggling was useless. She went limp—and concentrated hard.

The men were speaking Spanish. They were heading toward the parking lot—Nancy recognized the sound of the gravel they were walking on. As her kidnapper swung her upright, Nancy caught a glimpse of the car. It was a limousine, long and dark, and the windows were tinted glass.

A rear door was jerked open, and Nancy was thrown inside. One of the men started to climb in behind her.

Nancy kicked.

She kicked with both feet, since her ankles were bound together, and she heard an agonized groan.

Before she could lash out again, another man wrenched open a front door. Then he leaned over the seat back and pressed the muzzle of a gun against her forehead.

He snapped out some rapid orders in Spanish. Nancy didn't understand much of what he said, but suddenly a blindfold was tied around her eyes, and another strip of cloth was tied around her mouth.

Then one word came to her, loud and insistent.

"Muerta!"

That was Spanish for *dead*. The warning was terrifyingly clear.

Chapter

Two

NANCY LAY HELPLESSLY across the backseat. A moment later, the seat sagged. One of the men had sat down next to her. The gun at her forehead was shifted to her temple.

Doors slammed. An engine roared to life. The limousine jerked into motion with unbelievable speed. Nancy held herself motionless, like a crouching cat preparing to spring. But she couldn't spring—not yet.

She had to be ready.

She had to stay alert and not give way to panic. She had to force her senses to be aware of every detail of the terrifying ride.

It was astonishing how much Nancy could

notice, even with her eyes tightly bound. The car's ride was very soft and springy, in spite of the fact that they were hurtling along the dirt lane. She figured that they were on the lane because the car was rolling across the same ruts she'd driven over earlier, and occasionally she could hear stones fly up to ping against the undercarriage of the car.

Then the limousine was jerked abruptly onto a much smoother road. Although the windows were shut and the air conditioning was on, Nancy was able to hear the sound of air rushing past the windows and the zoom of other cars shooting by. That must mean they were on the interstate. They had turned left at the end of the lane. That meant they were heading toward Alexandria.

Nancy concentrated hard, counting in her head. How long was the ride taking compared to her drive to the college? Could she estimate the car's speed and therefore the mileage?

The limousine came to an abrupt stop, then made another left turn. It was heading toward the Potomac—toward Washington.

It made another turn, this time to the right, and was caught up in the roar of commuter traffic. Nancy thought they might be on Route 7 or the Belt Parkway.

Then, with a rush of terror, Nancy heard the roar of jet engines close at hand.

The airport! They're going to take me on a

plane! Nancy thought with panic. But the jet sounds receded. A metallic rumble underneath the wheels seemed to indicate that the limousine was crossing a bridge. Into the capital itself?

The limousine rattled over cobblestones and drew to a stop. A rush of fresh air and the lightening of weight on the seat told Nancy that a back door had opened and her seatmate had climbed out.

The next thing she knew, she was being dragged out and stood up. Something cold touched her ankles, and then the ropes around them were removed. Still gagged and blindfolded, her arms bound, Nancy was half pulled, half pushed, across an expanse of gravel and through a door. Footsteps echoed hollowly on cement.

There was an ammonia smell in the air, and once, when Nancy stumbled, her face brushed against something that felt like a cardboard carton. Were they in a warehouse?

A hand knocked on a metal door. The door was opened, and Nancy was dragged inside.

The voices of Nancy's captors, speaking in Spanish, became deferential. They're speaking to their boss, Nancy realized. But what are they saying? The Spanish was so rapid, so staccato, that she could only understand one word in ten.

Suddenly she was dragged over to a window.

Nancy knew it was a window because she could feel the warmth of sunlight against her cheek. Hands grasped her face roughly, turned it this way and that. Fingers ran through her hair.

Abruptly she was released—so abruptly that she lost her balance and fell painfully to the concrete floor.

Before Nancy could scramble away, a new set of hands grabbed her. Somebody's knees pinned her down as her ankles were tied again, this time with something cold and harsh. After that, Nancy was ignored.

Something was wrong, she realized instantly. With a cold fury, her captors' boss was yelling at them in rapid Spanish. Nancy recognized one or two insults that brought hot color to her face. Fortunately, no one seemed to notice. She was virtually forgotten until suddenly she was picked up and swung like a carpet roll over somebody's shoulder again.

The thugs rushed Nancy back outside and dumped her in the car.

Again the car jerked to life. Nancy forced herself to remain alert and clearheaded, but she could hear only an occasional word from her abductors. At least there was no gun at her head this time! Or could that be because there was something worse in store?

How long the second ride was, Nancy couldn't guess. She wasn't concentrating as hard as she had the first time, and it seemed that the driver was retracing his route. There were the sounds of traffic and the sounds of gravel.

Then the limousine lurched off the road into—what? A field? The car slowed. A back door was opened, although the car was still moving. Nancy's bound hands were pulled away from her body roughly. Something hard and cold touched them. Something stung her flesh. A knife. But it wasn't meant to hurt her. It was cutting her bonds.

Suddenly, with brutal force, Nancy was pulled up and then pushed toward the open door. She fought back with her freed hands, bracing her feet against the back of the front seat.

Voices were raised in Spanish. One phrase leaped out. "They could be twins!" Then a hand pushed the hollow of Nancy's back with professional accuracy. She fell, rolling and jouncing, onto hard ground that seemed to leap up to meet her.

Doors slammed and the car roared away.

Nancy was rolling and rolling, over rocks and grass. At least she wasn't on a road. She didn't try to stop herself until she was sure the limousine was far away. Then, shaking, she sat up as best she could and pulled the blindfold off her eyes.

She was sitting in the middle of a field, and

above a rim of evergreens rose the banner of Loudon College!

Nancy's heart, which had been pounding, began to calm down. At least her captors had had the decency to return her to where she had been snatched from. Clearly, it had been a case of mistaken identity, but who could the intended victim have been?

It was not the time to think about that. The sun was already low in the sky. With stiff fingers Nancy worked the handkerchief free from her mouth and spat out the gag that had been thrust inside. Her mouth was dry and raw, and she could hardly swallow. Then she attacked the bonds around her ankles. No wonder they had hurt! They were made of thick wire, the ends twisted around each other, and were so tight that her ankles had already swollen slightly around them.

At last Nancy was able to pull the wires free. She folded them carefully and looked around. Her purse! What had become of her purse?

The dark blue pouch with its shoulder strap lay only a few yards away. So it, too, had been thrown out of the car. Nancy tried to scramble to her feet, but her legs wouldn't hold her. The welts where the wires had been throbbed agonizingly. She crawled over to the small duffel bag and zipped it open. Her eyes narrowed.

The bag had been searched! Nancy knew

very well she had put her car keys in her change purse, but she pawed through her bag and found them loose on the bottom.

Those men seemed like pros, but they were either new at this or careless, she thought.

Nothing inside the purse had been taken. Nancy stowed the wires, gags, and blindfold inside and zipped the bag carefully. Then, with difficulty, she pulled herself up by holding on to a nearby tree.

I have to make sure I look all right before I see anybody, she decided.

If she walked slowly, she could manage. Gingerly, Nancy made her way out of the field and then along the lane and through the parking lots, leaning against cars for support. She checked her watch and was startled to see that it was only a quarter to five. The afternoon tennis matches were still going on.

A glance at her reflection in a glass door brought Nancy up short. She was a mess! She was looking in the same door she'd gone through an eternity earlier, and she saw what she'd missed before: steel letters on the wall beside the doors. Holling Gymnasium. This must be where the players dress. And if there's a locker room, there are showers, Nancy thought with relief.

She opened the door. The two security guards she saw scrutinized her government pass

carefully before waving her on. Nancy made her
way along the empty corridors until she found
the locker room and the showers.

Safely in one of the stalls, Nancy pulled the
heavy plastic curtain shut and stripped off her
clothes. She showered quickly, trying to keep
her hair dry, then bathed her injured ankles in
cold water for several minutes. Afterward she
dried off with a towel she'd grabbed from the
supply table and dressed again. Fortunately,
she'd been wearing cotton socks, and when she
pulled them up the swelling in her ankles didn't
show much. After applying a dab of lip gloss,
Nancy made her way outside.

Forcing herself to walk as normally as possible, Nancy went slowly toward the tennis
courts. She followed some other spectators
down a flagstone path to the entrance gate.

Then she saw something that made her stop
abruptly. She was so startled that it took a few
moments before she realized what the woman
at the gate was asking. "What? Oh, yes . . . I
have a box-seat ticket. It's here somewhere."
Even as Nancy searched through her purse and
handed over her ticket for the afternoon
matches, she was staring at the large display
board next to the entranceway.

It was covered with pictures of tournament
players. One of them was an action shot of a
player leaping into the air to return a lob.

Except for a difference in tennis style and slightly darker hair, the girl in the photograph could have been a mirror image of Nancy herself!

The realization struck Nancy all at once. She had been snatched coming out of the players' dressing area, wearing clothes that could easily have been mistaken for a tennis outfit. She had been kidnapped in error, mistaken for someone else. And that person, very likely, was the young athlete pictured flying into the air to smash back her opponent's shot!

"Nancy!" The loud voice was unmistakably George's, and right on top of it came Bess's. "Nancy, where have you been? We were worried sick!"

Her two friends were hurrying toward her from the grandstand. "Bess has been having a fit," George said anxiously. "Especially after we phoned the hotel and the woman at the desk said she thought you'd left a couple of hours ago. What happened?"

Around them, people were staring curiously. "Something came up. Tell you about it later," Nancy said quickly. It wasn't the place to share her experience, particularly if her suspicions were true. The best place for Nancy and her friends was in their box seats, where they'd be in full view of the crowd—and where Nancy would have a good view. She intended to keep a sharp eye out for the reappearance of her kidnappers.

"Let's go watch the tournament," she said brightly. "How much have I missed? Any cute guys around, Bess?" Nancy hoped the question would divert Bess from any probing questions of her own.

"Never mind that right now," George interrupted. "Teresa Montenegro's first game will start any minute. I don't want to miss it." She hurried the other two to a corner aisle and up the open wooden steps to their end box.

"Boy, was I glad to see you," Bess chattered, settling into her seat. "With all the security guys prowling around this place, I was beginning to be afraid . . . which is pretty silly, isn't it?" she finished, laughing.

"Shh!" someone in the box behind them hissed loudly.

Nancy turned toward the court. Her mind was racing. "All the security guys prowling around"—what did that mean? As everyone else watched a well-known American player walk briskly onto the court, Nancy caught George's arm and whispered the question to her.

"Because of Teresa," George whispered back. "Her country's a dictatorship, you know. I overheard somebody say there's been a bomb threat."

"Here?" Nancy asked, shocked.

George nodded. "There even were people picketing in front of the tennis stadium. This is the first time San Carlos has ever sent an athlete to an international competition. Some big shot from her government's coming to D.C. this week just to watch—and a lot of people don't like it."

With effort, Nancy kept her face from betraying anything. The San Carlos diplomat wasn't just coming to watch Teresa play. He would be here to meet with Senator Kilpatrick's top-secret committee—that was what the senator had told Nancy on the phone the night before.

All at once a roar went up from the crowd, followed by loud applause.

A slender figure of about Nancy's height was walking onto the court. Nancy saw the girl's eyes flick back and forth apprehensively as she moved past the rows of spectators. Her light brown shoulder-length hair caught the last rays of the sinking sun.

"That's Teresa Montenegro!" George said excitedly. "Hey, she looks a little like you, Nan, don't you think? Her mother was Irish, you know. That's where Teresa got her light hair and blue eyes."

As George chattered on, a chill ran down Nancy's spine. She had never seen Teresa before, but somehow she knew what she was thinking, knew the way she would leap in the air to return a high-bouncing shot—and knew why she was afraid.

Teresa Montenegro was the girl in the photograph, the girl who was the image of Nancy Drew!

Chapter

Three

N<small>ANCY, THIS IS</small> incredible," Bess suddenly exclaimed, turning to Nancy. "Teresa Montenegro is almost your exact double!"

"Almost, *nothing*," George said. "Now that I look closely, she could be your twin sister!"

Nancy's gaze never left Teresa as she responded, "We look enough alike . . . to confuse anyone . . . even professional . . ."

Afterward, Nancy was able to remember very little of that first match she watched Teresa play. Her eyes were too busy scanning the crowd for possible threats. Her mind was too busy piecing things together.

First I'm abducted, and then I'm dumped because a mistake was made, Nancy thought. No, that's not first. First there's Senator Kilpatrick and her mysterious committee, and the senator's calling me to do a secret errand. Then the snatching. Now here's Teresa looking like me—and looking scared. And the bomb threat!

Teresa had to be the connecting link between the pieces. I have to see Teresa, and fast, Nancy decided.

As soon as the match ended, with Teresa winning, Nancy began pushing her way out of the box.

Before she was at the bottom of the wooden staircase, George and Bess had caught up with her. "What's going on? Talk!" George ordered.

"Not here! Keep up with me till we find an open space." Nancy started to run toward the gym with the other two close behind. "Find out if Teresa's gone in there yet," Nancy told George, who took one look at Nancy's taut face and obeyed. Without being told, Bess slid the binoculars off Nancy's arm and began to watch the approaching crowd.

"Teresa's just leaving the field with a cute guy. They're walking this way," she reported just as George reappeared.

"Great. Then we have a few minutes." Nancy led them a short way from the gym to a deserted patch of open lawn. In a low voice and with as few words as possible, she told them about her abduction and her suspicions.

George whistled. "Have you called the police yet? . . . You've got to," she said when Nancy shook her head. "Even if Teresa's not in danger, something's going on! You can identify those men."

"From the way they acted, I think they're professionals, but they're inexperienced—or they'd have made sure who I was before they grabbed me. It might be a good idea to let Senator Kilpatrick know what happened before I call the police." Nancy broke off, her eyes narrowing.

Teresa and her companion had reached the road. They crossed it, so deep in talk that neither of them looked up. Just as well, Nancy thought. The "cute guy" was the stunning dark-haired, dark-eyed athlete who had let Nancy cut through the gym building earlier. But instead of entering the building, Teresa and the young man veered around it and headed toward the parking lots.

Nancy turned to Bess and George. "I have to warn her. You two meet me back at the hotel. There's a shuttle bus from here that you can take. Okay?" She sped off after Teresa and her companion.

By the time Nancy reached the parking lot, the two athletes were already ahead by several rows of cars. Nancy saw a group of fans stop the San Carlos girl for autographs. Almost immediately the man with her pulled her away from them. Then, still holding her, he began to run toward the next lot.

Another abduction? Nancy picked up speed. Suddenly, as they stopped beside a blue car, he released Teresa's arm.

Teresa abruptly turned to throw her arms around his neck.

Nancy's mind eased a little. From the way the two were kissing, it was clear that they were in love. It was also clear that they were in a hurry, and she thought Teresa looked a bit frightened. He unlocked the driver's door and, instead of going around to unlock the other, motioned for Teresa to climb behind the wheel and then slide over. She obeyed.

As the man climbed into the driver's seat, Nancy began to run. She was able to reach her rented car and gun the motor before the athletes' blue car nosed its way to the lot exit. But instead of turning toward the main road it swung into the lane, heading straight toward Nancy.

It passed her and zoomed down the dirt road, traveling at high speed.

Nancy swung her car into a tight three-point turn and took off after them.

The two cars bounced onto the highway and

headed in the direction of Alexandria. Soon they were swallowed up in homebound traffic. Nancy began a skillful game of cat and mouse, trying to stay only one or two cars behind the blue car. She couldn't afford either to lose them or to alarm them.

They passed the Tyson's Corner shopping mall and the skyscrapers of Crystal City. National Airport loomed ahead of her, then lay behind. At last the blue car was rolling, exactly at the speed limit, along Washington Street.

It turned a corner with a screech of the wheels—and swung into the driveway of the very hotel where Nancy and her friends were staying.

Nancy followed the car into the underground garage and parked several spaces away. Was her raincoat still in the backseat? It was. She pulled it on and thrust on sunglasses. They might look ridiculous, but they'd keep Teresa's companion from recognizing her. What Nancy had to say to Teresa she meant to say in private.

Her hopes of getting into the elevator with the two athletes were defeated. The young man pushed the Close button as soon as he and Teresa were inside. But Nancy had noticed the mirrored back wall of the elevator car, and she watched which floor button he pushed. Hoping that the elevator would get held up at the lobby, she tore up the emergency stairs and was loitering in the third-floor corridor as the two stepped out.

They hurried down the corridor and around a bend. As she pretended to unlock the door to one of the rooms, Nancy saw them exchange a few words. They seemed to be arguing. Teresa shook her head. Then she rose on tiptoe to kiss the young man—hard—broke off to unlock her door, and slipped inside.

The handsome athlete strode rapidly down the hall toward Nancy. As soon as he passed her, Nancy ran to Teresa's room, pulling her glasses and raincoat off as she did so. She knocked sharply.

After a moment a guarded, Spanish-accented voice replied, "Who is it?"

"Housekeeping. I have your extra towels." Nancy was glad she'd noticed that the hotel didn't provide many. She hoped that through the peephole her knit top would look like a maid's uniform to Teresa.

After what seemed like minutes, Nancy heard the sound of a dead-bolt lock being thrown. A chain clinked. Then the door opened wide enough for a stack of towels to be passed through.

Nancy and Teresa looked straight into each other's eyes.

Teresa's expression turned from surprise to

fear—and then to shock as she realized the strong resemblance between them.

At that moment a loud yell came from the direction of the elevator. It was followed instantly by the rapid fire of an automatic pistol.

Chapter

Four

INSTANTLY NANCY SHOVED Teresa back into her room and slammed the door shut. "I'm a detective. I work for the U.S. government." Nancy spoke in Spanish, as rapidly as she was able. If she didn't quite work for the federal government, working for a senator was the closest thing to it. "Stay inside! Lock the door and don't open it till I come back and say, 'It's Nancy. It's okay'!"

She saw comprehension flood Teresa's face, and as she dashed off she heard the door lock. Nancy turned the corner and came to a complete stop in front of the elevator.

The corridors in both directions were empty. The red lights on the plaque above the elevator showed that the car was going down, down, all the way to the garage level before it stopped.

It was too late to catch whoever was on the elevator. Nancy scooped up the house phone on the console table opposite the elevator door. "This is an emergency! Send someone from Security to the third floor right away!"

As she dropped the receiver Nancy detected a faint moaning. Her heart pounding, she traced the sound to a room scarcely fifteen feet away. Should she wait or take a chance?

If someone was wounded, there was no time to lose. Nancy hammered on the door, then tried the handle.

"Just a minute, miss!" A heavy hand closed on Nancy's shoulder. As she jerked around, the burly man produced his badge. "Security. Suppose you explain what's going on."

Quickly Nancy identified herself. "I'm a guest on the floor below. I phoned for you because I heard shots—right here by the elevator, I'm sure. And I just heard moaning from beyond this door."

"There's no moaning now," the house detective answered skeptically. Sure enough, the third floor was as quiet as a tomb. "From the second floor, are you? What were you doing up here, anyway?"

"Visiting a friend," Nancy said briefly. "And

I did hear shots!" Rapidly Nancy scanned the walls and floor around the elevator. Suddenly she dove beneath the console table. "Look at this," she exclaimed as she straightened up. "It's a spent bullet. A nine-millimeter, isn't it?"

The detective's eyes narrowed. "You heard moaning? As if somebody'd been hit?"

"I'm not sure. It was very weak, but there doesn't seem to be any blood around here."

The detective knocked on the door. "Security! I'm holding my badge up to the peephole for you to see. Open the door or I'm coming in with a passkey!"

The door opened slowly. "Oh, thank goodness. I've been so frightened," a small, white-haired woman said weakly. "I tried to call the front desk to tell them, but my hands were shaking so—"

"Tell them what?" Nancy asked gently.

"Why, about the kidnapping—" The little woman stopped, gasping for air. Nancy steered her to a velvet chair as the detective went to the bathroom for a glass of water.

"Drink that, and try to tell me. I'm sorry, ma'am, but it may be important."

"Yes, I know." The woman sipped some water, then went on. "I'm Mrs. Sherman. Mrs. John Sherman, from Atlanta. I was taking a nap before dinner. And I heard pushing and shoving coming from the hall outside. Then somebody screamed. I suppose I shouldn't have, but I—I opened the door a crack. I was afraid it was children playing, you know, and that one of them was hurt. So I looked out—"

Mrs. Sherman swallowed hard. "That's when the shots came. And I saw three men—no, four. One of them had the gun. He was pointing it at a nice young man while the two others were shoving him into the elevator." She spread her hands. "I would have helped him if I could! But it was happening so fast—they fell into the elevator, and the door slammed, and then I—I started having a dizzy spell."

The detective strode to the telephone. "This is Dixon. There are a couple of patrolmen having coffee in the coffee shop. Get them up to Room Three-twenty-two pronto!" he ordered. Then he turned back to the woman and took out a pen and notepad. "Do you think you can describe the men you saw?"

"Oh my, yes," Mrs. Sherman said firmly. "One of them was your size, and the other two were a little shorter. They were in their twenties, I would say. The bigger one, the one with the gun, was older. They all had olive skin, and one of the young ones had a small mustache. The other had a scar on his face. They were wearing dark pin-striped suits."

Nancy almost gasped. The descriptions fit her own kidnappers exactly!

"And the victim?" Dixon prodded.

Mrs. Sherman's eyes filled with tears. "He

was such a nice young man! One of the tennis players, I think. At least, he wore whites and some kind of badge. Beautiful dark wavy hair." Nancy recognized the description even before the woman added, "I've seen him before, with that tennis girl who's staying down the hall."

First an attempt to kidnap Teresa—now a successful kidnapping of her boyfriend! Now what do I do? Nancy wondered, perplexed. Tell what I know, or wait till I've talked to Senator Kilpatrick? For all I know, national security could be involved!

Before she could decide, the room exploded into action. Two young patrolmen arrived. Pushing her way between them was a forceful, middle-aged Hispanic woman.

"What is happening? I am Señora Ramirez, chaperon for the San Carlos entry in the international tennis tournament, and I demand to know! If there is danger, I cannot allow my charge to stay here!"

At that, everybody began talking at once. The police took down Nancy's story, or as much of it as she'd revealed to the man from Security. One of the patrolmen went up to the room on the other side of the hotel where Roberto—Teresa's boyfriend—was staying. Detective Dixon and Mrs. Sherman tried to calm Señora Ramirez. The police demanded to see Teresa. Señora Ramirez demanded that the police first provide an official Spanish translator and somebody from the San Carlos embassy. Then she took off in the direction of Teresa's room while the police made the necessary phone calls.

Nancy discreetly left the room. Not waiting for the elevator, she ran down the emergency stairs, two at a time, to the second floor.

George and Bess jumped up as Nancy entered. "Another kidnapping! This time it's Teresa's boyfriend. I have to call Marilyn Kilpatrick," Nancy said as she ran for the telephone. Before she reached it, George had dug into Nancy's purse and brought out the telephone number.

The senator wasn't in her office. She was in conference somewhere, and whoever answered the phone did not know when or where she could be reached. "Tell her Nancy has to talk to her *soon,*" Nancy said urgently. She didn't feel secure about leaving a more explicit message.

"I think you'd better deal us in," George said quietly as Nancy put down the phone.

"I think so, too, even though I'm not supposed to without permission." Nancy took a deep breath. "I'm supposed to receive a message from a courier in the Hollins Gymnasium locker room. Originally it was for this afternoon. Then the meeting was changed to tonight. I don't know what it's about, but it has to do with San Carlos. Senator Kilpatrick is involved in a secret top-level diplomatic mission."

George whistled. "Do you suppose it has

something to do with the attempt to kidnap Teresa?" she asked.

"I think so. Teresa's staying in a room one floor above us but facing the back. At least the police are with her." Nancy glanced out the window. "No they're not! Those two down there by the patrol car were the ones who talked to me, but they're leaving, and they don't have Teresa or Señora Ramirez with them." Nancy stopped, thinking.

"Bess, stay here in case the senator calls. Tell her what happened. George, come with me. The sooner we get some answers from Teresa Montenegro, the better."

Nancy and George ran for the emergency stairs. They were running so fast that George crashed into a dark figure who was on her way down. It was Señora Ramirez, out of breath and distraught. She grabbed Nancy and began shouting at her in Spanish.

"Please! Speak more slowly," Nancy pleaded, also in Spanish.

"Señorita Montenegro—she is my responsibility, and she has tricked me—"

Nancy finally understood that Teresa had asked her chaperon for some aspirin. While the older woman was in the bathroom getting it, Teresa had slammed the door shut on her and run out.

"She is going for the car I have rented. I know it. She took the keys—"

"We'll get her. Come on, George!" Nancy shouted.

They sprinted down the stairs and headed for the parking garage, leaving Señora Ramirez behind.

The garage was dim with shadows, lit only by a few overhead bulbs and the twilight coming in through the exit and entryway.

"Split," Nancy whispered, gesturing for George to take the left side. George nodded. Her tennis shoes made no sound as she ran.

A banner hung over the center parking area. It read International Women's Semi-Pro Tennis Tournament. Someone was doing a good job of promotion, Nancy thought briefly as she threaded her way to the right lane.

Something moved. Was it—yes, it *was* Teresa, furtively hurrying toward a car. Nancy started to run.

Then, all at once, a car engine roared to life nearby. Headlights glared blindingly, and Nancy saw the great shape bearing down on her—and on Teresa!

With a burst of speed, Nancy flung herself at the girl from San Carlos, knocking her down. Teresa screamed. At the same moment, Nancy wrapped her arms around Teresa tightly and jerked to the right. The two of them rolled over once, twice, as the car screamed by in a dark blur, just inches away from them.

"Nancy!" George shouted.

"Here!" Nancy called back. In that split second she must have let down her guard. Suddenly Teresa broke free, kicking Nancy away and leaping up.

As she did so, the dark sedan suddenly whipped into a turn and bore down on her again with incredible power.

Nancy scrambled to her feet. But there was no way she could reach Teresa in time.

Chapter

Five

TERESA FROZE, PARALYZED in the blinding light. Suddenly a figure leaped into the air.

George's strong arms caught at the tournament banner. It broke away, coming down with her, and was flung onto the front windshield of the sedan.

The car swerved crazily to the left. It bounced off the front fender of a sports car and tore erratically toward the exit.

The banner slid off in a little heap as the sedan, burning rubber, roared up the ramp and then vanished.

Suddenly the garage seemed very silent. The

only sound was the gasping sobs coming from Teresa, lying crumpled on the floor. Nancy and George ran to her, but she shrank away from them like a wounded bird.

"It's all right. I'm Nancy . . . Nancy Drew," Nancy murmured reassuringly, stroking the hair back from Teresa's frightened eyes. Teresa nodded, recognizing Nancy's voice. There was a large bruise like a rope burn on her cheek. She must have skinned it on the concrete when she fell.

George, an expert first-aider, checked Teresa for other injuries. "No damage except bruises," she reported.

"No thanks to whoever was driving that car," Nancy said grimly. "Teresa, somebody tried to kidnap me this afternoon. Yes, probably mistaking me for you," she said as Teresa's blue eyes widened. "Why is somebody trying to kill you?"

Teresa jerked her head away, pressing her lips together. George's eyes met Nancy's. "The same guy who shot at your boyfriend? They got him, you know," George said brutally. "That's what the racket was in the hallway, Nancy told me. If you won't talk to save yourself, how about him? We're on your side," she went on more gently as Teresa cried out. "Nancy can help you if you'll let her."

Nancy put her arms around Teresa as she

struggled to sit up. "Find Señora Ramirez and tell her Teresa's safe," Nancy told George in a low voice. "And brief the house detective. His name's Dixon."

George nodded and left. For a few minutes there was no sound except Teresa's ragged breathing.

"Don't you think you owe me at least some explanation?" Nancy asked presently. "After all, I almost got killed twice today because of you." As she hoped, that approach brought a response.

"I am so sorry. I do not know, really." Teresa swallowed hard. "It is—how do you say? A night scare?"

"Nightmare," Nancy supplied. "Teresa, you must think. There has to be a reason." No answer. "Why were you running away? From the police? From your chaperon?" She repeated the words in Spanish because Teresa seemed too distraught to understand.

"Not running away . . . Roberto? You said Roberto is dead? He can't be!"

"George didn't say that. He was kidnapped—probably by the same men who grabbed me. There was a witness. And there were shots fired. Roberto may have been killed, but we don't know yet. Teresa, don't you think you'd better—"

Teresa was shaking her head violently. "No!

There was a phone call—" She stopped abruptly.

"Teresa, *tell* me!" Nancy needed the facts before the police showed up and chased her away.

Teresa looked at her for a long moment. Then she nodded. "Someone called," she whispered. "Not Roberto—it was a message from Roberto."

"In English or Spanish?"

"Spanish. It said Roberto was hurt and needed me. He wanted me to come to get him."

"Where?"

Teresa gave an address in Alexandria. "I knew Señora Ramirez wouldn't let me go. She was hired especially to watch out for me on this trip, and she is very strict. She thinks I should have my mind only on my tennis game. So I . . . I tricked her."

"Didn't you realize how dangerous it could be?"

Teresa just looked at Nancy. "In my country, there is always danger. We have a dictatorship, very harsh—and often there are troublemakers from outside." She shrugged. "Roberto needs me. I must go."

"Not now, you can't," Nancy said firmly. *"I'll go."*

As she said it she remembered with a start that she also had to meet Senator Kilpatrick's mysterious courier soon. Nancy knew she needed to make sure Teresa was safe, then go after Roberto before it was too late. With relief, she saw Dixon and one of the policemen coming toward them.

"We'll take over now," the policeman said. He and the house detective led Teresa away.

Nancy returned to her suite, where George and Bess were anxiously waiting. "We're going with you," Bess said promptly when Nancy described her evening plans.

"Somebody has to be here in case the senator calls."

"I'll stay this time," George said.

"What you'd better do is order in some pizza for around ten o'clock," Nancy suggested, changing rapidly into the requested T-shirt, skirt, and red belt. "Looks as if none of us is going to get any real dinner. Come on, Bess."

With Bess holding a map and acting as navigator, Nancy cruised through the factory area on the outskirts of Alexandria, looking for the address Teresa had given.

"Either you heard her wrong or Teresa was supposed to meet her boyfriend in the Potomac River," Bess said at last.

"Maybe that's exactly what somebody had in mind," Nancy answered. "We'd better head for the tournament. Bess, go to your seat and stay there. Something dangerous is going on. If I don't show up by nine-thirty, send help!"

An amber moon was shining as they drove into the Loudon College parking lots. Nancy was fortunate to find a space close to the gym. She went with Bess to the box and leaned well forward in it, directly into the stream of light coming from nearby floodlights. It seemed a good way to advertise her arrival to whoever was watching for a girl in a denim miniskirt and a red belt.

At ten minutes to nine Nancy made her way to Hollins Gymnasium and used her pass to get in. Fluorescent lights glowed in the corridors, but the place seemed deserted. Nancy's running shoes squeaked spookily on the stone floors.

Cautiously Nancy entered the locker room. She was glad she'd been there earlier for that stolen shower. She knew her way around, knew the hiding places to watch out for—or to take refuge in.

The locker room was like all locker rooms— dim, full of discarded clothing, the smell of disinfectant and athletic equipment, the sound of water dripping from a faucet somewhere.

Nancy sat down on a gray wooden bench that gave a good view of all the doors and waited.

The overhead clock, obeying some class-session programming, rang noisily at 9:10 and again at 9:15.

No one came.

At twenty-five after nine, a door squeaked distantly. Nancy stiffened. Then she relaxed. It was no courier—apparently a match was over, and players and their chaperons were returning. They went directly to the shower room, ignoring Nancy.

Casually Nancy left the locker room and hung around for a few more minutes in the light directly outside the entrance of the gym.

I'd better get back to the box before Bess sends out the Marines, she decided.

Clearly something had interfered with the scheduled meet. And Senator Kilpatrick would have found a way to notify me here if she'd known, Nancy thought. She found Bess, and they headed for the parking lot.

It was a good half-hour before they were able to get out of a traffic jam.

"If we don't get there soon, that pizza's going to be stone cold," Bess grumbled as they barreled toward Alexandria.

"That will ruin your appetite?" Nancy asked absently. Instead of rising to the bait, Bess looked at Nancy's anxious face and remained silent.

When they entered the suite, George made the same comment. "It's ten-forty-five. The pizza's going to taste like wallpaper paste by now. And I ordered all the good stuff—turns out there's a Neapolitan pizza place nearby."

She stopped abruptly. "Something's gone wrong, hasn't it?"

"I hope not," Nancy said soberly. "Whoever was supposed to meet me didn't. I don't know what scared him off. Any word from the senator or Teresa?"

"Nope," George responded. She went to the phone and ordered another pizza.

They were still eating, sitting cross-legged on Nancy's king-size bed, when midnight came.

"The senator won't call now." Nancy's shoulders sagged.

"Be glad. Under these circumstances no news is good news," George pointed out. She sank her teeth into onions and pepperoni. "What I'd like to know," she went on around a mouthful of cheese, "is why somebody snatched Teresa's guy. Just to have a reason to lure her to the garage? Or did they really want to get her to the river?"

"It could have been a fail-safe setup," Nancy said thoughtfully. "If the first guy didn't run her down in the garage, he or a buddy would have a second chance over there. Believe me, nobody'd have known till morning. That neighborhood was dead." Nancy shuddered at her own choice of words. "What I'd like to know is why the police aren't doing anything."

The others stared at her.

"Think about it," Nancy insisted. "They don't know that I got snatched. But they do

47

know Roberto got snatched. With bullets bouncing around! And that somebody tried to run Teresa down in the garage."

George whistled. "I see your point. Have we ever known a situation like that when the place wasn't immediately crawling with cops? Especially considering the protests, the bomb threat, and the fact that a foreign sports figure's involved."

Especially considering there are top-secret talks involving the San Carlos dictatorship going on, Nancy added silently to herself. She had a lot of questions to ask Senator Marilyn Kilpatrick!

At last Nancy and her friends fell asleep. Before Nancy knew it, she was awakened by a brisk knocking at the main entrance to the suite. Nancy propped herself up on one elbow, noting that the hands of her clock stood at ten minutes to six.

Nancy jumped out of bed and ran to the door in her blue nightshirt. "Who's there?" she called softly.

"Marilyn Kilpatrick," a distinctive, familiar voice replied.

Quickly Nancy manipulated the chain and dead-bolt lock, and Senator Kilpatrick slipped inside. Nancy beckoned her into her bedroom.

"Sorry. I didn't mean to scare you, but I also didn't want to be seen coming here." Senator Kilpatrick's auburn hair was as smartly styled as always, but there were circles under her dark eyes. For once she looked every bit of her forty-eight years. "What happened last night? Why didn't you get the packet for me? Tell me quickly."

"A lot happened. And no, the courier didn't meet me." Nancy pulled on a robe as the senator sank down in a chair. In a few accurate sentences Nancy briefed the politician on the events that had occurred. Then she looked squarely into the dark eyes.

"You brought me into this. I think I've earned the right to be told more. Otherwise I could make a wrong move."

"You're right." The senator walked to the window and stood looking between the cracks of the blinds that Nancy had lowered. Then she turned.

"There ought not to have been any danger— to you or anyone else. But the—information exchange—is far more important than I've been free to tell you. What I'm going to tell you now I should not be saying to anyone who doesn't have top security clearance. I'm trusting you because I trust your father."

"It has to do with a possible revolution in San Carlos, doesn't it?" Nancy guessed.

Senator Kilpatrick nodded. "My committee is mediating between representatives of all the different political groups in San Carlos. We're hoping to avert a bloodbath. *Someone*—we're not sure whether from San Carlos or an outsider —does want one. I've been able to arrange for some very dangerous information to be smuggled to me. That's why I needed you."

"Not just because I'm Carson Drew's daughter. Because I look like Teresa Montenegro," Nancy said.

"Yes. Truly, I didn't think either of you would be in danger. I thought that the fact that you resemble Teresa would give you easy access to the gym, and if anyone saw you and the courier together no one would think anything of it."

The pieces started to fall together. *"Roberto* was the courier, wasn't he?" she said.

The senator nodded again. "And now we don't know where either he *or* his smuggled information is. If it falls into the wrong hands—" She didn't finish.

"Who is Roberto, really?"

"He's Teresa Montenegro's tennis coach. Also her boyfriend—or at least he has been for the past three months. He was the one who persuaded her to sign up for this tournament. He's also a leader in the underground freedom movement in San Carlos. I don't know whether she's aware of that. He may have felt she'd be safer if she wasn't."

Senator Kilpatrick paused. "I'm sure you know about the bomb threat and the protests. What you don't know is that the San Carlos dictatorship has drawn up a hit list. On it are the names of six people now in the United States who are actively working to overthrow the current government. Unless I get that list, and get it to the FBI within the next few days, those people will start to die!"

Chapter

Six

Nancy gasped. "There has to be a way to protect those people! Can't the FBI—"

"They can't do *anything* without the list of names," Senator Kilpatrick said starkly. "Nobody can. That's the terrible truth."

"Did Roberto have the list on him when he was kidnapped?" Nancy asked.

"I'm sure he's too shrewd and too aware of the danger to be carrying the list till he was on his way to meet you," the senator replied. "Even then it probably wouldn't have been recognizable and readable."

In code, Nancy thought.

"Whether he'd give it away after he was captured—" The senator stopped speaking for a moment, and her face turned pale. "That, I imagine, will depend on his strength. During revolutions, couriers have often carried secrets with them to their graves."

She was talking about torture. Nancy felt sick. "Aren't the police doing *anything* to trace Roberto?"

"This is a classified government matter," Senator Kilpatrick said bluntly. "It's not for the local police." She rose. "However, the government agencies can call on them when necessary. I'm going to arrange for you to have a police bodyguard."

Nancy groaned, and the senator's lips curved slightly. "He won't be obvious! I think you'll like him. I'm going to request a plainclothes detective who's been assigned special duty with me before. He's a go-getter, just out of the police academy. He'll fit right in with you and your friends."

"Two things," Nancy said resolutely. "I can't keep my friends in the dark about this. They've been pulled into it—they've got to know what's happening. They're totally trustworthy, they're smart, and they're experienced at helping me. But they won't be able to know how to help unless they have the whole picture."

After a moment's thought, the senator agreed. "What's the other thing?" she asked.

"Just how much danger do you think I'm in?" Nancy wanted to know.

"Not much, I hope. You're too visible now. Those goons who snatched you by mistake won't try *that* again. If they'd wanted to kill you, they'd have done so then."

"Which means," Nancy said, thinking aloud, "that they're not worried about my being able to identify them."

"They've probably been imported from San Carlos, or from some other link in the terrorist network. I'll find out whether it would be useful for you to look at mug shots or help a police artist make a composite drawing. Even if the men were imports, they may be known by the FBI or the CIA or Interpol, the international police organization."

"What do you want me to do in the meantime?" Nancy asked.

"Do exactly what you'd be doing anyway. Go to the tournament. I have a box there myself. I'll meet you there, and I'll bring along a young 'staff assistant' I want to fix you up with. I'm sure you and Dan can make that look authentic if required." The senator rose. "Any other questions?"

Nancy shook her head.

"Good." Senator Kilpatrick slipped out of

the suite, after carefully surveying the corridor for onlookers.

By that time George and Bess were quietly moving around in their own room. Nancy knocked on their door. "Phone down and order up breakfast, will you?" she asked. "I'll come fill you in as soon as I've showered."

Half an hour later they were once again having a mealtime conference, this time on George's bed. Bess and George looked somber as Nancy reported her conversation with the senator. "Poor Teresa," Bess said softly. "Think how she must feel—Roberto's both her boyfriend and her coach."

"Think how she'll feel having to walk out there on that tennis court today," George said realistically. "All it would take is a sniper up on top of the grandstand."

Bess repressed a shudder.

Following instructions, the three girls drove out to the campus as if nothing unusual were going on. The United States flag, the flags of the players' countries, and the Loudon College banner fluttered bravely against a robin's-egg-blue sky. The souvenir stalls and food stands were selling their wares; people were laughing and talking and watching players warm up on the side courts. A few tired-looking protesters waved their signs in the background, under the watchful eyes of the campus cops. There didn't seem to be any more security forces around than usual. Is the FBI here undercover? Nancy wondered.

While George strode off "to case the players," as she put it, Nancy and Bess went to their box. To Nancy's surprise, there were Marilyn Kilpatrick and a brawny, deeply tanned young man. "Nancy, hello!" Senator Kilpatrick said warmly. "Your father told me you were going to be here, so we stopped by to say hi. This is my staff assistant, Dan Prosky."

Nancy performed introductions. Bess took one look at the handsome young undercover detective and turned on all her charm. Meeting Senator Kilpatrick's suddenly dancing eyes, Nancy knew that the planned script was about to be rewritten. Apparently Bess was going to be the one Dan would fall for—and Nancy didn't think either of them would have to do any pretending. Not that she minded.

George, returning from her survey, also sized up the situation promptly. "Superjock," she muttered knowingly as Dan led Bess off for yogurt shakes.

Nancy grinned. "Since when have you looked down on athletes?" she teased.

"Only when they have such huge egos they think their muscles automatically make them supermen. Something tells me that's the case here. How come he's leaving you alone in the box?"

"In case somebody's trying to meet me." Nancy was wearing her meet-the-courier outfit with the identifying red belt, just in case. "Anyway," she said, glancing around, "I'm not exactly alone."

It was hard, in the atmosphere of cheerful excitement, to believe that a dangerous terrorist game was going on under cover of the tennis matches.

Dan and Bess came back, and the first match of the day—between Canadian and Japanese players—concluded. Nancy checked her program. Teresa wasn't scheduled until the afternoon. "I think I'll wander around awhile," she said.

"Mind if Bess and I come along?" Dan asked promptly.

"Of course not," Nancy replied. But once they were out of the area of the stands, Nancy turned to face them. "Look, the person who was supposed to meet me may find a way to show up—or someone else may come instead. But no one will come near me if I'm not alone. Can you keep up the surveillance from a distance?"

"Sure," Dan said. There was a new note of respect in his voice.

For the rest of the morning, Nancy prowled

the area behind the bleachers and around the gym. She carried a small camera and snapped pictures, both as a cover and in hopes of capturing clues.

The morning matches ended. The crowds streamed toward the parking lots and food stalls. Nothing had happened. Nancy, Bess, George, and Dan ate salads and drank iced tea in a pleasant outdoor restaurant. A few players and their coaches appeared there also. But not Teresa.

Afternoon came. It was time for Teresa's second match. Nancy and her friends watched the action closely. "She's good," Dan said. "Wouldn't know her mind was on anything but the game, would you?"

George's eyes narrowed. "She's not at top form. She was better yesterday. There aren't so many slashing serves today."

All the same, Teresa was able to maintain a slight margin over her opponent, a young German woman. What was remarkable was how she was able to do so with her distinctive style. Teresa seemed to thrive on difficult shots. She would miss easy returns and fall behind, then rescue herself just in time with a dazzling display of driving shots from the back corners of the court. And of course, there were her flashing leaps and powerful slams.

"Well, we may look alike, but our games are

certainly different," Nancy whispered to George. "She's much, much better than I am—that's for sure."

"You do okay yourself," George said consolingly.

The match had almost reached the end of the second set when Nancy became aware of three figures making their way up the wooden stairs to the row of boxes: A middle-aged woman with auburn hair—Senator Kilpatrick—followed by two men in dark suits, who Nancy assumed were from the Secret Service.

The senator stopped at the entrance to the box and spoke in a low voice. "Nancy, I need to speak to you. Alone."

Without a word Nancy rose. At a signal from the senator, Dan, Bess, and George remained in the box.

The senator led the way straight to a small concrete building just inside the players' restricted area. It was empty except for a file cabinet, a desk, and a few chairs. "The tournament committee uses this as an office," Senator Kilpatrick said, noticing Nancy's surprise.

After checking the room, the senator's guards shut the door and took up posts outside, leaving Nancy and the senator together.

Nancy was beginning to feel uneasy. "Something's happened."

Senator Kilpatrick's eyes were anguished.

But when she spoke her voice was absolutely level and emotionless.

"I've just been over at the hotel where one of the San Carlos delegates to my committee's conference is staying. Security people there found a body in the hotel garage. It was Roberto. He's been murdered."

Chapter
Seven

For a moment the closeness in the room made it hard to breathe. Distantly, applause and roars of approval came from the tennis courts. Somewhere near at hand a bird was singing.

Then a faint breeze came through the window and broke the spell.

Nancy wet her lips. "How was he killed? In the hotel gunfire?"

Senator Kilpatrick shook her head. "He was strangled—with a rope—sometime during the night." She paused. "The medical examiner said there had been torture."

"Then he might have given away the list."

"It's possible," the senator said quietly.

All at once, despite the summer heat, the room was very cold. "Poor Teresa," Nancy said at last. "Who's going to tell her?"

Senator Kilpatrick looked at her directly. "*We* are. On behalf of our government, I'm going to assure Teresa that we'll help her return home, or remain here for the rest of the tournament, as she wishes. You saved Teresa's life. I believe she trusts you. Definitely more than she trusts anyone else around here. I want you with me when I tell her that she has to be questioned."

"You don't think *Teresa* had anything to do with Roberto's murder!" Nancy exclaimed.

"I have no reason to think so. But she may be the only person who can give us clues that will prevent more murders. She doesn't have diplomatic immunity to protect her from being questioned. If she'll consent to it willingly, it will avoid a lot of . . . unpleasantness. For all of us."

In other words, Nancy thought, the government wants me to persuade Teresa to spill the beans. Whatever they are!

If she did, it might save Teresa herself from further danger. Nancy stopped short. Had someone intended to kidnap Teresa as a lever to make Roberto talk? Or had it been the other way around? That was something she'd have to think about later. At the moment, Teresa was playing her heart out on the field, while United States government agents waited.

"I'll help you tell her—if you wait till her match is finished," Nancy said firmly.

"There's no reason to spoil that," Senator Kilpatrick agreed. "We don't want to attract attention, anyway. You've met Teresa's official chaperon, haven't you? Point her out to me. I want to make sure she's not around when I talk to Teresa."

The request would have seemed unkind, but Nancy remembered the overprotectiveness she had seen yesterday in Señora Ramirez's behavior. She probably wouldn't let Teresa say more than two words, Nancy thought.

Nancy and the senator went back to the playing area, escorted by the Secret Service agents. The match was nearing its close. "That's the woman," Nancy whispered, pointing with her program toward a black-dressed figure in the stands. Had Señora Ramirez already heard about Roberto's death, or did she always look as though she were in mourning?

Senator Kilpatrick spoke quietly to the nearest agent. Within seconds, two business-suited government men were edging their way toward Teresa's chaperon.

As the match ended—another win for Teresa amid a roar of applause—Nancy saw the two close in around Señora Ramirez and steer her toward an exit at the other end of the grandstand.

Teresa came striding toward the path to the gymnasium, shouldering her way almost obliviously through a throng of well-wishers. She was wiping her dripping face with a towel, and the look in her eyes was remote.

Nancy stepped in front of her. She had to speak twice before Teresa heard her.

"Oh, Nancy. Yes. Did you enjoy the match?" Teresa asked in Spanish.

That was not the real question she wanted to ask, and Nancy knew it. "No, I didn't," Nancy said directly, and she saw Teresa flinch. She tucked her arm through one of Teresa's, as Senator Kilpatrick did the same on the other side. "This is one of our American senators, and a good friend," Nancy said gently. "We need to talk to you."

Secret Service men were deftly surrounding the three women and moving them in a unit toward the little concrete office.

As soon as the door was shut, Teresa looked at Nancy. Her eyes were dry. *"Muerto.* He's dead, isn't he?" she asked.

Nancy nodded. "Yes, he is. I'm so sorry. Teresa, we need your help to catch Roberto's killers. Senator Kilpatrick will explain about it."

"First, I must know how he died," Teresa said.

She listened stoically as the senator recited the story. "I do not know why it happened," she insisted as the senator questioned her gently. "All the time, in my country, there is killing. I did not think that could happen here."

"Could the other killings in your country have anything to do with your friend's death?" Senator Kilpatrick pressed. "Could they be connected to Roberto's murder?" The older woman repeated the question in Spanish to make sure it was understood.

Teresa's eyes flashed. *"No!* All Roberto cares about is tennis—and me!"

She was speaking in the present tense, Nancy noted with a pang. The realization must have struck Teresa, too, for the girl suddenly froze. Her eyes widened. Then, abruptly, she bent over sobbing.

"Give me a few minutes with her," Nancy whispered to Senator Kilpatrick. The senator nodded and slipped out. Nancy wrapped her arms around the slight, shaking figure and helped Teresa into a chair. She knelt beside her, holding her.

"I am sorry," Teresa said at last, straightening up again.

"Don't be. You have a right to cry," Nancy said.

Teresa shook her head faintly. "What you ask about Roberto . . . He has been my tennis trainer for three years, but my—what do you American girls call it?"

"Boyfriend?" Nancy suggested.

"My boyfriend three months only. Three wonderful months. We talk about so much. Never about politics. Never about governments." Teresa glanced at Nancy. "Since I am young, I have love for him. Why should we talk about politics?"

"What did you talk about?"

"He was so kind," Teresa said vaguely. "So romantic. He gave me a book of poetry just before we came to America. . . ."

Senator Kilpatrick came back in, followed by her bodyguards, and at once the atmosphere became businesslike. The authorities—which ones? Nancy wondered—had already searched Roberto's locker in the men's gym and his hotel room. Now, said the senator, they wanted to search Teresa's too, just to see if he'd left anything there that could give a clue. Her chaperon was currently being questioned, but Teresa could ask to have her present for the search if she wanted.

Teresa shook her head. "I prefer to have Nancy Drew."

The Secret Service men exchanged glances and shrugged. Together they went to the Hollins Gymnasium locker room, where Teresa's belongings were searched. Then they drove back to the hotel, where her room was searched.

An agent found the book of poetry, in Spanish, with its Spanish inscription signed by Roberto. He put it down, looking bored.

"There could be a clue in that," Nancy said to him quietly when Teresa could not hear.

"If there are any coded messages around, we'll find them," the agent said condescendingly. "It doesn't look as though your South American friend needs you anymore. We want to have her take a look at some photographs at our office, and the lawyer her embassy's sending over will be all the moral support she needs."

Nancy bit back the retort she felt like making. She gave Teresa a last compassionate smile and went downstairs to her own suite. Bess and George were there waiting for her.

"Bess has been making time, as usual," George said dryly after Nancy had told them what had happened and confessed how little she really knew.

Bess blushed. "I just told Dan how wonderful it must be to have a really *significant* job like the one he has and to know what's *really* happening behind the headlines. Don't laugh!" she said hastily, as the others grinned. "I'm not just leading him on. I really like him! Good looks *and* brains, for a change! But I thought I ought to use mine and do some detecting, too."

"What did you find out?" Nancy asked.

Bess pulled off her sundress and carefully laid out a less casual outfit while she answered Nancy. "I got a lesson on South American politics. That president-for-life in San Carlos really *is* bad news. He'd probably arrest someone for looking at him cross-eyed, and so many people have simply disappeared that the place is on the edge of a real revolution. And our government's going crazy because there's no knowing which political group will take over! Meanwhile, back at the palace, the president's bought himself some terrorists to eliminate the leaders of the opposition. And there are probably other terrorists trying to eliminate *him.*"

"You can't tell the players without a scorecard," George murmured.

Bess nodded. "According to Dan, the players are switching sides all the time. He says that every time you blink, people change loyalties there.

"Well, I'm first for the shower," Bess continued, heading for it. "You two had better get a move on. Dan's picking us up for dinner in half an hour, and he's bringing along two more bodyguards."

"Who's going to protect us from them—or them from Bess?" George wondered aloud.

Bess was right—Dan was good company. He was intelligent, shrewd, and funny, and so were his friends. They ate dinner in a Greek restaurant, and afterward there was music and dancing. It was a fun evening. Or it would have been, if Nancy could have gotten Teresa off her mind.

But she was still thinking about her when the young men returned the girls to their hotel. "Want us to see you into your rooms?" Dan asked.

"Thanks. I think we'll be safer if you don't," Bess answered with a laugh.

The men walked the girls to their door anyway and waited until they were safely inside. George bolted the door.

"That was a nice evening. I think I'll check with the front desk to see if there were any phone calls while we were out," Nancy said, heading for her own bedroom.

She flipped on the light switch as she entered. Then she screamed.

Chapter

Eight

THE SCREAM BROUGHT Nancy's friends running. They froze, appalled, their eyes following the direction of Nancy's pointing finger.

There *was* a message, but it hadn't come by phone and hadn't been left with the front desk. It lay in the center of Nancy's bed in the tightly locked suite.

It was a doll, an eight-inch redheaded doll with a teenage figure, dressed in an abbreviated blue bikini. The doll's head lolled sickeningly to one side. A red cord was knotted around the broken neck.

A note was attached, written with a blood-red marker:

GO HOME, SEÑORITA.
THIS COULD BE YOU!

Nancy recovered quickly and approached the bed as Bess dove for the phone.

Bess frantically punched numbers, then spoke in a rush. "Dan! Get back up here fast!" She dropped the receiver with a clatter that made them all jump.

"So he just happened to give me his beeper number," Bess said with a forced smile as Nancy eyed her. "It's a good thing he did." She reached out toward the broken doll.

"Don't touch it!" Nancy jerked Bess's hand away. "There may be fingerprints."

Footsteps came pounding down the corridor. "They sure didn't waste time waiting for the elevator," George commented, opening the door carefully with her hand wrapped in a section of her skirt so she wouldn't leave prints.

All at once the room was full of very stern plainclothes detectives. Dan borrowed Nancy's small camera to take pictures as his friend Joe phoned for reinforcements. The girls weren't allowed to touch anything in the room until a fingerprint expert had arrived. When he came, FBI agents were with him.

"Where are we supposed to go?" Nancy demanded when the fingerprint man refused even to let her sit on the edge of the bathtub.

"If you have any sense, you'll go back

home," Dan told her flatly. "This is no mess for nice girls like you to be mixed up in."

"*Teresa's* mixed up in this mess," Nancy replied with conviction. "I'm not leaving until she's out of it. There has to be some way I can help her! And I'm not going home until Senator Kilpatrick has that hit list in her hands!"

She turned to her friends. "There's no reason you have to stay here, though. Why don't you phone home? I'm sure Dan can find someone to take you to the airport."

"No way!" George said gruffly as Bess nodded loyally.

"All for one and one for all?" Nancy whispered. "Thanks, guys."

"There's one thing you *are* going to do, whether you like it or not," Dan said, reaching for the phone as the fingerprint expert finished with it. "I'm under orders to protect you, so I'm moving you out of these rooms. I happen to know the government's paid the hotel to keep the rooms on either side of Teresa's empty," he added as he punched the button for the hotel manager.

Nancy was about to protest, but she stopped abruptly. That location would be perfect! Within minutes, the three detectives were helping the girls carry overnight bags up the emergency stairs.

"No one will know you're in here," Dan said with satisfaction as soon as he'd checked out the new two-bedroom suite. "I told the manager we're using these rooms for a stakeout. We'll move the rest of your things up tomorrow. In the meantime, you can lie low." He thumped the pillows on the living-room sofa. "And I'll spend the night right here to make sure nobody bothers you."

Nancy nodded silently. She had her own plans in mind—plans that would be blown if Dan spent the night on the sofa. He'd see her leaving the suite.

Then her brow cleared as a thought struck her. If this suite was set up like the one they'd just left . . .

"I'd really like to freshen up," Nancy said demurely. "Did anyone bring a blow-dryer?"

"I think I brought mine," said Bess, picking up her bag.

"Let's get everything sorted out in here," Nancy said, leading the way to the far bedroom and firmly closing the door.

"What was that all about?" George demanded suspiciously.

Nancy put her finger to her lips. "Turn on the dryer," she whispered. "I don't want Dan to hear us." Then, followed by George and Bess, she tiptoed straight to the phone. She punched the number of Teresa's room.

On the second ring, Teresa answered, her voice a tight whisper.

"It's Nancy. Are you alone?"

"No, but Señora Ramirez is asleep in the other room," Teresa replied softly.

"Well, I'm in the room on the other side of you. We just moved in here. As soon as I put down the receiver I'll unlock the connecting door on my side. You lock the door between you and Señora Ramirez and come in here."

In less than a minute, Teresa stood in the connecting doorway. Her eyes were swollen with weeping, and she looked very frail in her thin nightdress. "Have you heard any more about Roberto?" she asked immediately.

Nancy hurried her inside. "We have to talk softly. Our bodyguard's in the room just outside this door. Didn't the government assign anyone to guard you?"

Teresa shook her head. "Now that Roberto's dead, they think I'm not important to the assassins," she said simply.

"I'm not so sure." Nancy sat on the bed opposite Teresa and took her hands. "I want you to think very hard. Tell me everything you can remember about Roberto's movements from the moment you arrived in Washington."

Bess flicked the record button on the little cassette player she often brought along on trips. George took the memo pad and ballpoint pen from the bedside table.

Teresa stared at the connecting door as if it were a TV screen on which she was watching a documentary of her journey. "So much was new—I have never been out of my own country before, so I remember—the plane came in—"

"Which airport?" Nancy asked quickly.

"I don't know. Near here—there was a lot of traffic, and we could see the dome on your Capitol." National Airport, Nancy thought. Good. It was only a mile or two away.

"We come out of the plane into a corridor like a tube. Then we go through a waiting area—we don't stop at all—and down a wide corridor with windows. Then we come to Immigration. They ask a lot of questions about why are we here, and stamp our passports. The man was nice," Teresa said with some surprise. "He wished me luck in my tournament."

"Then what?" Nancy asked.

Teresa described a routine the girls all recognized. Down an escalator. Waiting endlessly for luggage to be unloaded. Finding luggage carts and suitcases—and, in Teresa's case, tennis rackets. Then the long ordeal of Customs inspection. The inspectors had been very thorough with Teresa and Roberto and Señora Ramirez. They had taken away the fruit Teresa had brought with her and the flowers she'd been given at the San Carlos airport.

Then the party had gone into the main lobby. They had not yet separated at all, not even to go to the restrooms. At that point, Teresa said,

Roberto had noticed how much Señora Ramirez's feet were hurting and had suggested she sit down.

All at once Nancy's ears perked up. "Where did Roberto leave Señora Ramirez?" she asked breathlessly.

"He left both of us," Teresa corrected her, "and went to find out about the car we had arranged to rent. It took him a long time, I think, but—"

"Did he go anywhere else?"

Teresa frowned. "I do not think so. It was a very long day," she confessed. "We had been traveling since dawn."

Nancy jumped up, her eyes shining. At last there was something she could do. "Bess, go into the sitting room and turn on the charm," she commanded. "We're going to the airport, and we'd better have Dan with us!"

"What? The airport *now?*" George said. "Why, Nancy?"

"I have a hunch that Roberto may have left the list there somewhere—and I want to find it before anyone else does!"

In a few minutes Nancy, Bess, George—and Dan—were in Dan's car, with Dan at the wheel. Apparently Bess had been very persuasive. Teresa had begged to go with them, but when Nancy had reminded her of her tournament match the next day, she had returned reluctantly to her own room.

Dan's small station wagon reassured Nancy. So did his own brawny presence. No one would connect him or his car with San Carlos or with Nancy Drew—particularly since Nancy was wearing Bess's sundress and George's battered baseball cap, both brought by Dan from the downstairs room.

Then why, Nancy asked herself as they rolled up the exit ramp from the parking garage, do I suddenly feel as if something's about to happen?

She found out all too soon. As the station wagon turned into the street and headed for the corner, a car parked near the curb came quietly to life. It pulled in behind them as they halted for the stop sign—then turned left just as Dan did.

"We're being followed," Nancy said quietly.

Chapter

Nine

Nᴏᴛ ꜰᴏʀ ʟᴏɴɢ," Dan replied grimly. He started cruising at a slow speed. Then, as they approached a traffic light, he slowed down even more.

The light began to change. Swiftly Dan slammed the wagon into gear and shot through, barely missing being hit by a sports car that had jumped the signal in the other direction. The sports car was not so lucky. Dan's pursuer smashed into its right side—and was then penned in place by the flow of traffic from the cross street.

Nancy watched, fascinated, as Dan roared

away. "Car pursuing police officer in accident on corner of Washington and Queen," Dan snapped into his car radio.

"Pretty smooth," George commented admiringly as Dan proceeded to execute a complicated series of turns and cut-throughs that brought them onto the service road to the airline arrivals building.

"Don't try a maneuver like that unless you're a cop on a chase. And even then you'd better have a darn good reason," Dan answered, grinning.

He parked in short-term parking, and the four threaded their way through sparse late-night traffic into the terminal. There they played back Bess's cassette recording and went over the careful notes George had organized so as to retrace Roberto's and Teresa's steps. Dan even got permission to go up to the actual tunnel through which the three travelers from San Carlos had deplaned.

"Nothing here," Dan remarked after searching every inch of the tunnel. "You find anything?"

"Only a piece of a baggage claim ticket." Nancy turned it over to him. "It's from an afternoon flight today. Not much use."

They searched the waiting area and worked their way down the corridor, still without discovering anything. Dan arranged to have the

Customs and Immigration officials who had been on duty at the time available for questioning in the morning. "The FBI boys will probably insist on doing that themselves," he said enviously.

At last they reached the main concourse again. Nancy looked around. "Where are the car rental counters?" she asked.

"Over there," Dan said, pointing.

"Then I'll bet this is the sitting area Teresa mentioned. It's the closest one. Now if we could just figure out where Roberto might have gone while Teresa and Señora Ramirez waited here. He'd have to be out of their sight for a while so he could look for a hiding place."

Nancy stood back as Dan began a careful search, alerting an airport security officer as he did so. Bess and George also began to search under Dan's direction, while Nancy just stood thoughtfully. The others glanced at her curiously, but she ignored them. There were times when working with her brain could bring faster results than hunting for clues.

He'd have known he wouldn't have much time, Nancy thought. He'd do what I'm doing— stand still for a minute and look around.

What would he have seen? The chairs. The standing ashtrays. They might be good places to leave something for pickup by a contact, but the meet had been planned for the tournament—not the airport.

Past the sitting area were a small coffee shop, which Dan was checking, and a novelty store. In the window was a large poster for the tennis tournament. Whoever's doing promotion for the tournament hasn't missed a trick, Nancy reflected, remembering the banner in the parking garage.

She sauntered over to look at the array of Washington, D.C., souvenirs in the store windows.

I wish I had a picture of Roberto with me to show the store owners, she thought. She'd have to come back with that later, after finding out when the same clerks would be on duty.

Where else could Roberto have gone to quickly, out of sight of Teresa? The restrooms?

"Negative," Dan reported, emerging from the men's room.

It seemed unlikely that Roberto would have risked going into the ladies' room, but Nancy checked it just in case. Also negative.

There was nothing left to investigate but the baggage lockers themselves. They could only be rented for twelve hours at a time. Roberto would have to have planned a trip back to the airport twice a day to check the merchandise—

Something's not adding up, Nancy thought,

frowning. I'm sure the airport was the only place Roberto could have hidden the hit list. Unless he had it on him when he died.

He couldn't have, or bodies other than Roberto's would have started turning up.

By then Dan and Bess had returned, followed soon by George. "Pretty smart to advertise the tennis tournament out here," George said, nodding toward the novelty store. "Should bring in a lot of tourists."

Nancy only nodded. She was still lost in thought. Bess slipped an arm around her. "Come on. Dan'll drive us home. He says the FBI will go through this place thoroughly first thing in the morning."

They headed for the car. It was waiting, locked tightly, just where Dan had left it. Before unlocking it Dan went over it from top to bottom with an electronic beeper. "Just in case," he said tautly. "Though a listening device would be more likely than a bomb."

Dan unlocked the car, and they climbed in quickly. He paid the parking fee at the exit gate and began driving around the spiral of roads that led to the Memorial Parkway. There weren't many cars at that time of night.

"Hey, that's the second time that big gray car's changed lanes with us," Bess said suddenly.

Nancy sat up straight. "What big gray car?"

Bess pointed. Dan stole a glance over his shoulder, and his eyes narrowed. "I've seen that car before tonight."

"I've seen it before, too," Nancy said. "If it's not the one I was kidnapped in, it's the spitting image of it!"

"Car rental company license plates," Dan noted. He read them out to George, who wrote them down. Then he radioed in to the police.

"Okay." Dan grinned humorlessly. "Let's lose 'em."

He put on a burst of speed. The gray car fell behind. Nancy remembered the speed it was capable of and felt a twinge of apprehension. But the car made no move to catch up with them, and her tension eased.

"Almost home," Dan said reassuringly to Bess, who cuddled close to him.

By then the parkway was practically deserted. That shows how late it is, Nancy thought drowsily.

Suddenly lights flashed in her eyes. No, not lights. Mirror reflection—

Nancy sprang up in the seat just as the big car bore down on them, ominously close.

"What—?" Dan yelped as the headlights, turned to high beams, hit him right in the eyes.

The gray car struck them from behind, and the little station wagon swerved with a sickening lurch.

Dan fought desperately for control. But before he regained it the killer car struck again, ramming the wagon toward the guardrail.

The lightweight wagon leaped into the air—and then crashed through the rail. It plunged down the steep embankment with Nancy and her friends inside.

Chapter

Ten

*W*HAT *DO YOU mean, you almost got killed in a car crash?"* Ned's voice shouted through the telephone receiver into Nancy's ear.

It was three A.M.—two hours after the accident. In that time Nancy and her friends had been rescued by patrolmen in a passing police car who had seen the wreck. Dan had succeeded in convincing them that it was all a classified government matter. Unfortunately, that had involved notifying Senator Kilpatrick.

While Dan was getting chewed out by his superiors, Senator Kilpatrick was on the telephone to Nancy's father, who chewed *her* out for putting his daughter in such a dangerous position. Then Carson Drew had spoken to Nancy.

"Dad, I'm all right," Nancy had insisted. "Dan did a wonderful job of getting the wagon under control. He got us out before the fire could start. We're all just fine!" Nancy said, rubbing one of several bruises.

"Things are far from fine," her father had interrupted. "Marilyn finally told me the whole story. I'm flying down tomorrow."

Soon after Carson Drew got off the phone, the much needed call came through from Ned. Nancy almost cried, she was so tired and so glad to hear his voice. But the note in hers only made Ned more worried.

"I'm coming down with your father," Ned said immediately.

"Ned, you really don't need to. I'll take care of myself, I promise. And if I don't, Dan will."

"The way he did tonight? Exactly who is that character?" Ned asked suspiciously.

Nancy laughed. "A very smart, go-getter jock who's a whiz kid for the local police and who—I think—is angling for a job with Senator Kilpatrick. You'd like him. And *he*," Nancy added with emphasis, "likes *Bess.*"

She was relieved to hear Ned laugh. "Okay, I get the message. Maybe I'm going overboard worrying, but I love you."

"I love you, too. And thanks for worrying. I'll call you if I need you, I promise."

"How about calling 'cause you want me?" Ned asked. Nancy laughed and put down the phone, feeling much better.

The next thing she knew, it was nine A.M., and Bess was shaking her awake. "The senator's on the phone."

Nancy struggled to a sitting position, still half-asleep. "Where is everybody?"

"George took the bus to Loudon to watch Teresa warm up for the afternoon match. Dan's gone out to buy a newspaper. He's already brought us breakfast. He didn't want room service to know anyone's in here. Nancy, come on! The senator's practically spitting bullets!"

Nancy reached for the phone.

"About time!" the senator's husky voice said crisply. "I want to see you. At the tournament. Be there by ten-thirty."

"Has anything more happened?" Nancy demanded.

"I can't talk." The senator hung up.

"You look awful," Bess said frankly, reappearing with a container of orange juice and a bag of doughnuts.

"What do you expect after we sat up talking till five?" Nancy bit into a doughnut, eyeing Bess. "I must say you've recovered remarkably. And you got even less sleep, I'll bet."

"Dan must be good for me," Bess said. "Nancy, go back to sleep for a little longer. You don't have to go to the tournament this minute. Teresa's got a whole gang of bodyguards."

"You mean the government finally came through?"

"Not ours. Hers," Bess said. "Roberto's murder also made the headlines down there. The San Carlos government's calling it a 'provocative international incident.' Their people are keeping surveillance on Teresa, and our people are keeping surveillance on them."

"Scratch the sleep," Nancy said resignedly. "I'm taking a shower and going out there."

By ten-thirty she was out at Loudon College, just in time to join George and watch the end of Teresa's workout. "This place is really crawling with cops today," George reported. "All types and all nationalities. Things are getting sticky."

"Tell me about it," Nancy retorted glumly, thinking about the hit list.

"If you ask me," George said decidedly, "Roberto's death was deliberate political murder."

"I agree," said Nancy. "But by which side? We don't even know for sure whether forces inside or outside San Carlos are responsible."

One thing was certain. Keeping everything hush-hush was rapidly becoming impossible.

Nancy looked around casually. Two college security guards were talking together at the far end of the court. Another stood near Nancy. Three U.S. government men were wandering around, looking out of place in business suits. Several Latin men were also gathered nearby. They were leaning against the wire fence, watching Nancy and George. Those must be the guards Bess had spoken of.

Nancy shuddered. She was beginning to wonder what fate Teresa's government had in store for her. The papers that morning had been full of rumors about how cruel and totalitarian the dictatorship was.

"*Buenos días,* Nancy." Teresa came toward Nancy and George, wiping her forehead with her wristband. She looked sad but composed. "How about hitting a few with me, George?" she invited.

"I'll get my tennis shoes," George said gladly.

Soon the two were exchanging rapid strokes.

"Your friend's in seventh heaven, isn't she?" a voice said behind Nancy's shoulder.

Nancy spun around.

Senator Kilpatrick stood there, elegant in a white linen dress and large brown straw hat. Beneath its shade her eyes were steely.

"What's wrong?" Nancy demanded, alarmed.

"Plenty, in my opinion. Don't worry, I don't mean with you. Come have an early lunch with me."

Nancy followed the senator to a small tent, plastic-walled and air-conditioned, that opened off the main dining tent. Iced tea, salad, and dessert were waiting, but the tent was empty, and the senator's own bodyguards stood outside.

"Something's going to happen, isn't it?" Nancy asked.

"I'm furious about what *isn't* happening," the senator corrected her. "I'm fully aware that this is a sensitive situation, but it's difficult to have a straightforward meeting with the representatives of the San Carlos political factions—which I'm supposed to be doing right now—when I'm not allowed to mention Roberto's name! Of course the people from San Carlos want to know what's going on—and what can I say?

"Especially when Roberto was known to be an opponent of the San Carlos regime *and* of U.S. foreign policy there," Senator Kilpatrick continued. "That was the reason he was smuggling the list to me rather than the CIA. He met me when I was on a fact-finding mission in San Carlos a few months ago, and he trusted me. He suspected that people in authority in both our governments were, if not aiding and abetting government terrorists, at least closing their eyes to them. I don't know if he was right, but it's terrible not being able to investigate it!"

"And the killings could start any time," Nancy added gravely.

The senator nodded. "I've just learned from a private source that a well-known hit man flew into Mexico from San Carlos yesterday. He's already left Mexico, supposedly for the Bahamas. But the plane makes stops at some American territories on the way."

"You mean he could be on the mainland already?"

"Right. Time's running out."

"What do you want me to do?" Nancy asked.

"I guess I'm hoping for a miracle," Marilyn Kilpatrick said frankly. "Your father says you've produced those before. I'm hoping you'll bring a fresh eye to this case, and a mind that's not bogged down in politics and routine."

"There must be a way to stop the assassinations—there has to be!" Nancy hardly realized she was thinking out loud. "Every criminal makes a mistake sometime. And Roberto was no fool. He knew he was in danger, so he must have planted that list somewhere it could be found if he was . . . taken care of. If only we had a little more time."

But time, as the senator had said, was running out.

They finished their lunch. Beyond the plastic wall Nancy saw George talking with some of the other players. From the glow on George's face, Nancy guessed they were complimenting her on her game.

"Let's go join her," Senator Kilpatrick said,

following Nancy's glance. They went out and followed George to the grandstand.

Just as George reached the gate in the high wire fence, a man came through it, heading toward the stairs to the boxes. Nancy gasped.

"What?" Senator Kilpatrick said instantly.

"He's one of the guys who abducted me. Call Security!" Nancy tore off, passing George as she did so.

Immediately George came running after her. She and Nancy raced up the steps and into the narrow aisle that separated the front and back rows of boxes.

At the far end, the man was sliding into a bleacher seat next to a man in a hat who was reading a newspaper. The newspaper was lowered briefly.

"I don't know him. But the first guy's one of the ones who snatched me!" Nancy whispered to George.

"Get down! He knows you by sight, remember?" George whispered back. "I can pass for just another player." As Nancy ducked, George began sauntering along the aisle.

She had almost reached the two men when the one in the hat folded his newspaper and looked sharply in George's direction.

Nancy's heart lurched. He was one of the ones who had been leaning against the fence watching Teresa's workout! He had seen George there with Nancy!

George must have recognized him at that same moment. She half paused, then changed direction, heading up the rows of bleachers.

As she did so, the two men also rose and began to run after her. So did Nancy. *If she can just get to the exit stairs!* Nancy thought. *If Senator Kilpatrick just brings help in time!*

There *was* no time. Everything was suddenly happening at high speed. George was running. The men were running after her. And Nancy was pounding after them, kicking off her sandals as she did so. Barefoot, panting, she scrambled after her friend—who was by now on the top row of bleachers.

George scrambled into the announcers' booth. Seconds later one of her pursuers was there, too. Nancy stumbled and went down, hard, on one ankle. She jerked herself up in time to see George hurtling out the other side.

All at once, the second pursuer stopped. Something glinted in his hand. There was a faint crack-pop.

He was shooting with a silenced gun straight at George's head!

As Nancy stared in horror, George did the only thing possible. With a gymnast's skill, she started climbing the pole that supported the electric scoreboard.

Up and up—George's only chance, Nancy knew, was to make a run for it along the top of the billboard. If she herself could distract the pursuers—

Gritting her teeth against the throbbing in her ankle, Nancy pulled herself upright and began to make her way rapidly along the aisle.

There were two more faint cracking sounds. But no bullets whizzed past Nancy. She whipped around—to see George, midway across the top edge of the scoreboard, lose her balance and topple helplessly toward the ground far below.

Chapter

Eleven

SOMEBODY SCREAMED. NANCY didn't wait to see who. She threw herself down and rolled under the bleacher seat, dropping to the ground. It was not a long drop. She looked around at once, expecting to see George's crumpled figure.

George was nowhere to be seen.

Several sets of legs raced along behind the bleachers and then stopped abruptly. Nancy crawled out and looked up, as the other spectators were looking.

High above, a figure clung to a slanting beam. The bleacher support had broken George's fall. George was all right—or at least right enough to grab the beam and hang on tight. Now she was working her way to safety as onlookers held their breath.

Instinctively Nancy's gaze swung higher. The pursuers were no longer using George for target practice. They were fleeing frantically as security guards closed in.

The guards were too late. The assassins got away. "But at least you're okay!" Nancy cried, running to hug George.

George grinned weakly. "It takes more than that to get rid of me." She brushed herself off gingerly, wincing as she did so.

College officials insisted on having George examined by the tournament physician before they'd let her leave. Then Senator Kilpatrick herself took George and Nancy back to the hotel in her government limousine.

"I hope this thing has bulletproof windows," George joked. To Nancy's secret relief, the bodyguard-driver answered quite seriously that it did.

Instead of pulling up at the hotel entrance, the driver drove directly into the underground garage. The second bodyguard stepped out and checked carefully before allowing the senator and her guests to leave the limo. They went directly into the elevator, accompanied by both guards, and took the elevator first to the top floor, then down to Nancy's, using a special key to keep the door from opening at an earlier stop.

Again, one guard stepped out first and looked around before motioning to the others to follow. He was also first around the bend in the corridor—and immediately he flung out an arm to hold the women back.

"There's a guy hanging around outside the Drew suite, and he looks like he means business!"

Nancy was already peering cautiously around the corner. A handsome man with a distinguished touch of gray at the temples was pacing in obvious fury. Nancy let out a glad cry and tore down the hall before the guards could stop her. *"Dad!"*

Carson Drew caught her in his arms and held her tight. All he said was, "Let's go inside," in a controlled tone that Nancy knew too well. Quickly she unlocked the door, and they all entered.

Carson Drew turned on the guards immediately. "I wish to speak to these ladies alone. Could you please take up posts directly outside the door?"

The authority in his voice carried weight. So did the faint nod Senator Kilpatrick gave. The bodyguards obeyed. Carson Drew bolted the door behind them and then swung around.

"What do you think you're doing risking the

lives of private citizens like this?" It was Marilyn Kilpatrick he was shouting at, not Nancy. "I agreed to a courier mission. Now there's been a murder, and these girls are attacked in broad daylight. I heard what happened at the tournament," he snapped as Nancy started to speak. "It came over the radio in the lobby. And there's a pack of reporters down there waiting to ask questions!"

"Dad, don't you think you could ask George how she is first, instead of yelling?" Nancy asked diplomatically.

Carson Drew caught himself. "I'm sorry," he said. "How are you, George? Is there anything I can do?"

"I'm fine, thanks. But I think I'll go soak my aching bones in a nice hot tub." George vanished discreetly.

Nancy and Senator Kilpatrick exchanged glances. "Dad, have you had any lunch yet?" Nancy asked. Not waiting for an answer, she went to the door and asked the guards to order something up. Behind her, Carson Drew and the senator began to exchange words.

"Carson, believe me, there was *no way* I could have foreseen that Nancy would be in danger. Or George—or Teresa Montenegro, for that matter." Something in Marilyn Kilpatrick's voice made Nancy's father grow sober and attentive. *"No one* knew Roberto was going to try to smuggle that hit list to me. No one other than the San Carlos dictator and his hit squad knew the list existed."

"Except this Roberto," Nancy's father retorted with irritation.

"Roberto knew because he was a member of an underground group trying to overthrow the dictatorship. A *moderate* group," she stressed. "He found out somehow and got in touch with me because we'd talked when I was down there some months ago. He was afraid if the word leaked out to the more radical rebels, or here in Washington, somebody might decide that the people on the list were expendable for propaganda value. He knew he'd be putting his life on the line smuggling the list to me, and he lost his life.

"But he didn't think Teresa would be in danger. A young female tennis star? She's one of the best publicity gimmicks her government has! So I thought Nancy would be perfectly safe posing as her for the few minutes that the contact would take."

"But Teresa's *not* safe," Nancy said aloud. "Why? And why did those guys shoot at George? Just because she played a practice game with Teresa? None of this makes sense."

Then she gasped. "Suppose they weren't at the stadium to follow any of us. Suppose they've decided *Teresa's* expendable! What you said about the people on the list—wouldn't the murder of Teresa Montenegro, while she's in this country and you're having those secret peace-making sessions, be the biggest possible provocation *against* peace? Especially if the other side, and the U.S. government, could be blamed? Please, call the FBI and have them search the stadium."

In the shocked silence that followed, they all heard the door of the other bedroom open. Bess stood in the connecting doorway. Her face was glowing, but her eyes were anxious.

"What have you been up to?" Nancy asked with effort. "Or should I say you and Dan?"

"We've been driving around, sightseeing, but—" Bess stopped and her glow faded. "What is it? You know, don't you?"

"George was shot at, and she fell off the top of the scoreboard in the process," Nancy said rapidly. "Don't worry, she's only bruised and shaken." Then she paused and looked at Bess curiously. "What do we know?"

"I'm upset, too. Give me a minute to catch my breath." Bess sat down on the bed, locking her hands together.

"Dan took me for a romantic drive around the tidal basin," she said wanly as the others waited. "Past the monuments and the Capitol . . . you know. He had the morning off because of the business with his car last night. We ordered him a new one. Brown," she added irrelevantly. "In the meantime he's using a car from the police car pool."

"All in all, you two managed to have a pretty good morning," Senator Kilpatrick said dryly.

"It started out that way . . . I *like* Dan," Bess wailed. "I really do. He's strong and funny and sensitive. He says just the right things."

"Or at least what you want to hear." Now George appeared in the connecting door, wrapped in a terry-cloth robe and turban.

"George, that's not fair . . ." Bess swallowed. "Senator, when he saw there were guards here he dropped me off and went to find you. We heard on the police radio that the airport police collared a pickpocket at the airport last night. He tried to bargain his way into a lighter charge by supplying information. He saw somebody arrive on a plane from the Bahamas. Somebody called El Morro."

Bess wasn't finished speaking, but at that moment a cry burst from the senator's lips. They all looked at her, but it was to Carson Drew she turned.

"Carson, that man's one of the most wanted terrorists on Interpol's list. He has a reputation for eliminating anyone who stumbles on to any clues to his existence, whether his current employers want him to or not. I'm sure he was one of the men who tried to kill George!"

Chapter

Twelve

NANCY, I CAN'T help worrying about you. I'm your father," Carson Drew said with a faint smile. Then his face grew serious.

"I'm proud of you for many things, and one of them is the way you never let personal sacrifice or danger deter you from doing what you believe is right. Or from helping someone who is in need. I admit there are times when I want to jump in and protect you from the consequences. And there would probably be more of them if I always knew what you were up to while you were up to it!

"I guess now I rely on my respect for your good sense and judgment. The trouble is, I also know that all the sense and judgment in the world can't always save us from the consequences of other people's actions."

"I know," Nancy whispered. "That's the way I've felt over Roberto's death. So helpless. And so—responsible for not having been able to protect him from it."

The Drews were alone in Nancy's hotel bedroom. Senator Kilpatrick, outraged that the news of El Morro's presence in the country had not reached her sooner, had been driven to her office in search of further information. She had left one of her bodyguards on duty. He was outside the door to the suite now. Bess was fussing over George in the other bedroom.

"Don't feel guilty," Carson Drew said sternly. "You're a human being, Nancy, not a computer or a comic-book heroine! Even computers can only act on the data that they have. Can you think now of anything you'd have done differently with Roberto, given what you knew then?" Nancy shook her head. "Then if you gave it your best shot, that's all anyone has a right to expect of you, even yourself."

Carson Drew tilted Nancy's chin up, making her look at him. "I meant what I said about being proud of you. I do understand why you do what you do. And I approve."

Nancy hugged him.

Just as her father's arms tightened around her in response, the telephone rang.

"I'll get it," Bess called. And then, "Nan, pick the phone up. Quick!"

The voice that came to Nancy was barely distinguishable as Teresa's. "I must see you alone. Can I come to your room right away?"

"Of course! I'll unlock the door between—"

"No. Go to your window. Quickly." The phone went dead.

"What is it?" Carson Drew asked at once.

"It's Teresa. She's in trouble, and if she sees you she won't talk. Dad, go to your own room—fast." Nancy fairly pushed him out. Then she ran to her window and threw it open wide.

A moment later a figure scrambled down the fire escape. It was Teresa, unrecognizable in a painter's cap and a maid's uniform.

Nancy pulled her in. "Teresa, what—"

"Shh!" Teresa slammed the window shut and pulled the drapes. "I sent Señora Ramirez out for souvenirs and postcards so I could get away. I remembered I saw these clothes in the service room yesterday, and I borrowed them. They are a good disguise, yes? No one will recognize me if I go out? I went up to the next floor and came down the fire escape. We must talk quickly. She may be back already."

"If she'd come back and found you missing, we'd have heard the shouting," Nancy said frankly. "Teresa, why do you need to go out?"

"I found a note in my locker when I went to change after practice," Teresa said.

Nancy's heart sank. If a note could be smuggled in there, so could a bomb!

"The note is from a—a *compadre* of Roberto's in the underground. He must see me. I am marked to die, and so are others." She lapsed into frightened Spanish. "Many others, not just the six—"

Nancy interrupted. "Teresa, listen to me! This could be a trap!"

Teresa shook her head violently. "No! He mentioned things no one not close to Roberto could know. The poetry book Roberto gave me—the message he wrote inside." She grabbed Nancy's arm. "This *amigo,* he wants to ask me questions. Questions that may give us a clue to some message Roberto could have left me!"

"I'll go with you," Nancy said at once.

"No, I must go alone, but that is not the problem." Teresa drew herself up proudly. "With Roberto dead, I do not care about the risk! I must find that list, or his death will have no meaning."

"Tell me what you want me to do."

Teresa leaned forward. "There is only one time this man can meet me. At six o'clock tonight. But Nancy! At six o'clock I must be at the tennis tournament."

Nancy frowned. "I thought your match today was earlier." She looked at her watch. "Right now, in fact."

Teresa cut her off. "It was postponed until tomorrow. One of my opponents took sick and must be replaced. The stadium will open again at five today, and at six I am to play a doubles match. Not part of the tournament. It is a benefit for the poor people in my country—an American man and I will play against the girl from Canada and her coach. Roberto was supposed to be my partner, but—" Teresa forced tears back sternly. "It has been advertised. How can I not show up there? How can I be in two places at one time? Nancy, help me!"

In two places at one time—Nancy looked at the girl from San Carlos, almost unrecognizable in the baggy uniform and the cap that concealed her hair. Aside from the suntan, she could have been Nancy herself in disguise.

"I know how," Nancy breathed. *"You* play the doubles match. *I'll* go to your meeting."

"Nancy, I told you you cannot—"

Now it was Nancy's turn to interrupt. "Wait a minute! I play tennis—not as well as you, of course, but I'm good. You said yourself it's a doubles match. I'll play in it for you—as Teresa Montenegro. And you'll go to your meeting—as Nancy Drew!"

Nancy tiptoed across the living room to the other bedroom. "Bess!" she hissed, opening the door. "Come to my room. We need you. You, too, George."

"I don't understand," Teresa whispered, bewildered, when the three girls returned.

"You will. Just listen."

Quickly Nancy outlined her brainstorm. It would require acting skill, but Nancy had that from many previous cases. And she was sure she could persuade Teresa to play *her* part. It also required alterations, not just of appearance but of mannerisms and of Nancy's tennis game.

George grasped the possibilities first. "I can coach you, Nancy. I've learned lots of Teresa's techniques, thanks to this morning's workout. I'll try to make your tennis look as much like Teresa's as I can."

"But what about little things like skin and hair color?" Bess objected.

"That's where you come in," Nancy said promptly. "You're the fashion and beauty expert. Run out and buy whatever's needed at a drugstore. Be prepared to give me a cut and blow-dry. Teresa, go back to your room before your chaperon pushes the panic button. I'll arrange to have her receive a diplomatic invitation she won't dare turn down. George, get on the phone to the senator. Tell her *we*"—she emphasized the word—"need the use of a tennis court that can provide *absolute privacy*. Tell her I'm testing out a theory, but don't tell her anything else."

As the other three sprang into action, Nancy sat down quietly. She felt as if the room were whirling.

Teresa's meet was vitally important—and this was the only way it could take place without alerting the terrorists. Of that Nancy was absolutely sure.

She was absolutely sure of something else as well. She had only a few short hours to complete the transformation—not just of her appearance but of her tennis game.

She, Nancy Drew, expert detective but amateur athlete, was about to play before a thousand or more people. Play against people good enough to be professional. Play well enough to carry through a triple deception—of the United States government, of the public, and of the San Carlos agents assigned to keep Teresa Montenegro in line.

Could she do it?

Chapter

Thirteen

THE NEXT FEW hours were among the most frantic of Nancy's life. Within ten minutes Senator Kilpatrick sent the "armored car," as George called it, to take Nancy, George, and Teresa to a private home somewhere nearby. The girls never found out who lived there, and no one was in sight, but inside the high walls around the grounds was a magnificent tennis court.

For two hours Teresa drilled Nancy in the characteristics of her tennis style, with George acting as coach to see if Nancy followed Teresa's moves precisely.

"It'll do," George said at last. "Nancy could

never pull off the substitution in a regular tournament match, but people will probably think your playing looks different because this is mixed doubles."

"Let's hope so!" Nancy said fervently. "My game's suffering because I'm concentrating so hard on copying Teresa's style. And I'd never have the stamina for a full match!"

"I would," George said regretfully. "I wish I could try it."

"Perhaps when this is over, you and I will have a chance to play together in another meet," Teresa told George gently. There was a moment's silence. They were only too aware that some of them might not come out of the afternoon's deadly games alive.

"We'd better get back so Bess can have her crack at us," Nancy said briskly.

The limousine sped them back to the hotel. Again they were whisked carefully inside, under heavy guard. Bess was in the suite, surrounded by hair and makeup paraphernalia. "I shortened Nancy's skirt so it'll be the right length for Teresa," she reported. "And I bought Nancy some tennis shoes like the ones Teresa wears. You guys should be able to fit into the rest of each other's clothes." She hurried them both into the showers to wash their hair.

The next hour was a hectic flurry of activity, with Bess presiding and George acting as her assistant. Bess and George applied bronzer to

Nancy's skin. "You'd better have it everywhere," George insisted, "since you'll have to change clothes in the locker room." Fortunately Nancy had some tan already, so the deeper color was not too much of a change.

After that, Bess—who was good at it—trimmed Nancy's hair, referring to Teresa constantly as a model. Then she began to apply colored hair gel lavishly.

When she finished, Bess had matched the girls' hair coloring quite well. Next she worked over them both with brush and blower.

Last of all came makeup. Bess relied mostly on Nancy and Teresa's own cosmetics, but she was also able to do some skillful work with light and shadow.

"Be glad of what I learned when I was in those school plays," Bess muttered, blending brown and lavender under Nancy's cheekbones. "Okay, take a look."

Till then, she'd kept Nancy and Teresa away from mirrors. Now they stared at themselves, amazed. Somehow Nancy's cheekbones had grown higher and broader, the bone structure above her eyes seeming a bit more full. On Teresa the effect was the reverse. Once dressed, each girl's resemblance to the other's normal appearance was uncanny.

"Now spritz your faces with this bottled water to set the makeup," Bess commanded. "No, wait! *I'd* better do it."

"You're not afraid this bronzer will run off?" Nancy asked apprehensively.

"Not till you scrub hard with soap," Bess said emphatically. "I tried it once. Believe me, I know! Once I was a South Sea islander for days!"

"It's time you two were going," George said, glancing at her watch. "Señora Ramirez should just be leaving for that cocktail party. How'd you arrange that?"

"I told Dad that Señora Ramirez could use an evening out after all that's happened. He knew just the right people to—" Nancy gasped. "We've been rushing so much I forgot to arrange transportation. Teresa can't drive into D.C. in our car—not in rush-hour traffic!"

"It's taken care of," Bess said. A troubled look crossed her eyes. "Dan thinks he's driving Nancy and me into Georgetown to follow up one of Nancy's hunches. After we drop Teresa off, we're going to have dinner at a place he knows. Then we'll pick Teresa up again."

"Good thinking," George said approvingly.

"I hate not being honest with Dan," Bess said. "But it was the only thing that I could come up with."

Nancy nodded sympathetically. "I know what you mean," she said, thinking of Ned. "But if you'd told the truth, it would have been Dan's job to stop us."

"I'll be able to keep Dan occupied so he

won't ask Teresa too many questions," Bess went on. "And the senator's sending some other bodyguards, who haven't seen either of you two before, to drive Teresa . . . well, actually *you*, to the doubles match. The senator agreed with me that Teresa might be safer without her San Carlos guards than with them, so she's arranged a way to spring her from custody."

"You didn't tell Senator Kilpatrick what we're doing, did you?" Nancy exclaimed. Instinct warned her the deception should be secret even from the senator. Especially after the way Dad lit into her earlier about jeopardizing our lives, she added mentally.

"I didn't tell *anybody*," Bess emphasized. "But I'll sure be glad when this is over."

"I, also," Teresa said somberly. "No matter how it ends."

There was a momentary silence.

The phone rang. It was Dan reporting that he was ready for the trip into D.C.

Teresa rose. Then, resting her hands lightly on Nancy's shoulders, she looked directly into her eyes. *"Vaya con Dios,"* she murmured. She picked up Nancy's handbag and slipped out into the corridor. Bess followed.

Ten minutes later George and Nancy left too, carrying Teresa's tennis rackets and gym bag. George sat in the front seat of the government car, beside the driver. "Teresa wants to be alone," she told the other bodyguard. "She's got to psych herself up for this match."

They rode out to the Loudon campus in absolute silence. Nancy was grateful that this limousine, like the one that had kidnapped her, had tinted windows. No one could look in at her, and in the Washington area limos were too common to attract much notice.

They reached the campus. Nancy noticed that the parking lot was well filled. Apparently many people had come to watch Teresa play and help the refugees from her country.

The limousine pulled up by the gym. To Nancy's relief, security police had made the place off-limits for all but the four players. In the women's locker room Teresa's Canadian opponent greeted her pleasantly but otherwise let her alone. Nancy changed into Teresa's favorite tennis outfit and put on the new tennis shoes. Fortunately they fit well. She propped Teresa's mascot, a small doll—a replica of a San Carlos Indian woman—beside her on the bench and gazed at it somberly.

Nancy was beginning to realize all too well just how easily the switch of identities could go wrong. I can't think about it, she told herself. I've got to psych myself into the game—into *Teresa's* game. She closed her eyes and concentrated.

All at once she heard a commotion in the

hall. There were the sounds of a scuffle, and then George's voice was raised wildly.

"You don't understand! I've *got* to see Teresa Montenegro!"

Nancy ran to the door. George was struggling with two guards in the lobby of the gym building. She caught Nancy's eye and signaled frantically.

It was a risk, but Nancy took it. She stepped out of the locker room and strode forward to reach out for George, her own eyes flashing imperiously as she'd once seen Teresa's do. "Let go of her!" she commanded.

To her great relief, the guards let go of George and stepped back—but only a few feet. They would never let George follow Nancy into the locker room out of their sight.

George turned her head so that only Nancy could see her lips. They formed the words almost soundlessly. *"Trouble. Bess phoned. Teresa phoned her at the restaurant. The big guy down south has ordered the execution of traitors everywhere to begin at dawn!"*

She emphasized the word *everywhere*. Nancy's eyes darkened. *"Teresa?"* she asked soundlessly.

George nodded imperceptibly.

The same thought was in both girls' minds. If the San Carlos dictator—the big guy—had ordered killings, there was no guarantee that hit men like El Morro would obey his decree that they should be carried out at sunrise. El Morro might not feel like waiting!

And by posing as Teresa in the doubles match, Nancy was putting herself in terrible danger!

Chapter

Fourteen

EL Morro, or another hit man, could be in the grandstand crowd at that very moment! For an instant that was all Nancy could think of. Then a man wearing the uniform and badge of a tournament official opened the door.

"Two minutes to six. To the courts, please, players."

George gave Nancy a swift, tight hug and hurried off. The young Canadian woman came out of the locker room and shook hands with Nancy, murmuring, "Good luck."

The two male players left their locker room. Nancy's partner was a cheerful-looking man in his early thirties, with sandy hair. "Sorry I didn't have the time to practice with you earlier," he apologized. "I was tied up with some last-minute coaching."

Nancy smiled and shrugged.

Escorted by tournament officials—and by security men disguised as officials—the two couples marched across the road and out onto the court. There was a burst of applause as they entered. Nancy smiled and nodded like the others, but involuntarily her eyes searched the crowd.

I have to stop that, she told herself. The best way to protect Teresa is to make people believe *I'm* Teresa!

The other couple won the toss and chose to serve.

The Canadian woman's first serve was deep and hard. Nancy's partner returned it well, but the Canadian coach hit a great shot down the line. Nancy missed it.

"Fifteen-love," called the referee.

Nancy knew within five minutes that the deception was going to be even more difficult than she'd feared. She was in a double bind. To play well, she would have to use her own style, and the masquerade would be exposed. But if she forced herself to play like Teresa, her reflexes were slowed, and she missed shots Teresa would have hit.

Once, after she'd netted one of Teresa's

characteristic backhand shots, Nancy caught her partner looking at her strangely. But the game was too fast for him to focus on anything other than his own playing.

The Canadian team took the first set easily.

George was at the rail when Nancy wearily went to her seat for the few minutes between sets. She was not allowed to enter the court, but her eyes spoke plainly to Nancy. *Calm down. Don't force so much! Zen.* Her lips framed the last word.

Nancy frowned. Then her face cleared. George was referring to the zen of a sport, a phrase Nancy had heard her use often. It meant concentrate on the objective, on the target, not on the technique you hope will get you there.

Nancy and her partner won the next game. A faint murmur reached her from the bleachers, and Nancy resolutely put away the fear that her own tennis style might be creeping in. Concentrate on where the ball should go, as George had said. Rely on the earlier practice for the style—

A gleam of light from somewhere in the stands danced into Nancy's eyes, and she missed a high volley, not even getting her racket on the ball.

There was a disappointed murmur from the crowd, followed by a ripple of appreciation as Nancy's partner ran in to save the shot, catching the ball on its first bounce. He slammed it back, and the momentum of the game picked up again.

The ball came toward Nancy, and she moved forward to meet it. But as she swung, the glint of light bounced into her eyes again. The glare was just great enough to throw her off-balance. She tripped and fell, scarcely hearing the referee's voice announcing the point for the other side above the groans of the crowd.

Pretending dizziness, Nancy knelt for a moment on one knee. But her eyes were busily sweeping the stadium.

The light had come from the far end—from the east. So it couldn't be rays from the dying sun. None of the tournament floodlights had been lit yet. Where was it coming from, and why couldn't she see it now?

Nancy's partner strode toward her, concerned about her delay. Nancy nodded at him and began to rise. Then she saw the glint again.

As if he knew she needed his help, Nancy's partner caught the next few balls with some dazzling maneuvers. There was no repeat of the flash of light, and Nancy was able to return some shots successfully. Her mind was racing.

If the glint was not from electricity or the sunset, what had caused it? Sunlight from behind her? Binoculars? A camera lens? A telescope?

Then the truth crashed down on Nancy. It

was a telescope of sorts—the telescopic sight of a sniper's rifle!

Nancy froze. A ball smashed past her, and the glint came again. Instinctively, Nancy ducked.

She made it look like a stumble, and murmurs rose from the crowd. Nancy's partner strode toward her. Nancy shook her head. And then, with sharp clarity, she knew there was only one thing to do.

It was the Canadian woman's turn to serve. As the ball came toward her Nancy completely abandoned her attempt to imitate Teresa's style. She rushed forward to meet it with a wild forehand slam that sent the ball soaring over the crowd—directly toward the sniper.

There were gasps from the crowd. They must have assumed Teresa was cracking beneath the pressure. But one person knew better. George's eyes had been on Nancy. They followed the ball. Then they swung back to meet Nancy's for a shocked instant, and the next moment George was grabbing the nearest security guard and pointing.

From all over the stadium, officials began to dash toward the sniper.

I did my best, Nancy thought. All I can do now is hope.

She rushed back into the game, and she did not see the telltale glint again.

Nancy played hard after that, with all her

skill. She knew the best thing she could do was to prolong the game and keep the Canadian pair from winning easily. She had to give Teresa as much time on the loose as she could.

"Game. Set to San Carlos," the referee called. The announcement was made over the loudspeaker. "The match is now a tie."

During the third set, Nancy and her partner played well. When it ended, they had lost the match by only two heartbreaking points in the last set!

The players shook hands. Exhausted, Nancy walked slowly from the court amid a flurry of whispers. The Canadian woman came over to put a companionable arm around her shoulders.

"You made a great comeback," she said. "Too bad you lost when the game was so close. That would have killed me!"

Nancy gave a tight grin. "You don't know how close it came," she murmured in her best attempt at a San Carlos accent.

Chapter

Fifteen

GEORGE MET NANCY with a quick hug as soon as she stepped off the court. "The sniper got away," she whispered at once. "Our driver's waiting right out front, and the other guy got your things from the locker room."

During a wild ride on the parkway, the driver abandoned the pretense of driving a private limo and used a siren. He turned it off once they were within half a mile of the hotel. All the same, Nancy and George were back in their suite just twenty minutes after the match ended.

Teresa was already there with Bess, and both

of them were distraught. The news about the sniper had come over the car's two-way radio as Dan and Bess drove back from the restaurant. Bess had been forced to tell Dan about the entire plot and masquerade. He had been furious.

"He said we were dumb and reckless—that not only could he lose his job as a result, but we might have caused either or both of you to lose your lives!"

"That is crazy," Teresa said sharply. "I knew the risk to me, and I chose to take it!" She looked at Nancy. "But it was not right of me to let you risk your life."

"Yes it was," Nancy said firmly. "How else could we have found out about the dawn executions?"

Then she looked more closely at Teresa. "What's wrong?" she asked in a concerned voice. "I mean, what *else* is wrong? What happened at your meeting with Roberto's friend?"

Tears welled up in Teresa's eyes. "I am sure it is not true," she whispered. "Or no—I am not sure. But—"

"But?" Nancy prompted gently.

"But this friend, he is telling me Roberto—Roberto was not to be trusted! That he was—what did he say?—a double agent, working for the dictator *and* for the revolutionaries. He says he found, in Roberto's papers back in San Carlos, some letters that show that he wanted to *sell* the list of names to the senator."

"Sell the list?" Bess gasped.

"Yes," said Teresa. "If she would not pay enough, Roberto would not care what happened to the people on the list!"

"So he really wasn't working to overthrow the San Carlos dictatorship?" Nancy asked, appalled.

"There is no way to tell *whose* side Roberto was on." Teresa bit her lip. "And maybe he would even betray me!"

Nancy was horrified, but there was no time to think over what Teresa had said. It was almost nine o'clock.

"Dawn's at five-fifty-seven," Bess said starkly. "The senator checked. Dan took Teresa straight to her as soon as he found out."

That meant Senator Kilpatrick knew about the masquerade—and Carson Drew probably knew as well. "Where's the senator now?" Nancy asked weakly.

"At the Department of Justice, pushing panic buttons and pulling strings. She took your dad with her," Bess added. "I almost forgot. She said that out of desperation the government agents even took Teresa's poetry book. They used microscopes and infrared light and tried all kinds of code tests, and it's clean. So Teresa will get it and that postcard she was using as a bookmark back tomorrow."

Nancy saw Teresa's face change.

"What postcard?" Nancy asked instantly.

Teresa shook her head, turning away slightly. "It is nothing . . . I just realized that that card is the last thing Roberto ever gave me," she confessed, wiping away tears.

"Roberto *gave* you a postcard?" Nancy jumped up. "Teresa, think hard. When did he give it to you? And why?"

Teresa looked at her, bewildered. "Why . . . when we were leaving the airport, Roberto said he wouldn't have time to write postcards, that he was stupid to think he would. He threw the cards into a trash can. And I—I said I would like to have the picture of the Capitol to take home to my mother. So Roberto laughed and took it out of the can and gave it to me. I was keeping it in the poetry book."

"Teresa, *think!* You'd just gotten into the U.S. You hadn't even left the airport! When and where did Roberto get American post-cards?"

Teresa frowned. "He must have bought them—"

"The novelty shop!" Nancy almost shouted. "I *knew* that must have something to do with this! It was the only place Roberto could have gone during those few minutes. He must have written a message on one of the cards."

She faced the others urgently. "Come on! We have to get hold of the manager of that store! The hit list may still be there."

"Hold on," George said promptly. "One, the store's been searched—several times. Two, he could have mailed the card. Three, and most important, the senator's not about to let any of us loose till the hit men are arrested. She gave strict orders to those musclemen outside our doors."

"That's easy," Nancy said. "George, phone the senator's office, tell her assistant that we need to follow up a lead for the senator."

Hiding a grin, George did so. "We're in luck all the way," she announced when she hung up. "We've got a bulletproof car and escorts, your father's occupied looking up legal measures the senator can invoke to protect the people who could be on the hit list, and your chaperon," she added, turning to Teresa, "has just been picked up by the FBI. It seems she has an interesting past they want to find out more about."

"Chatty assistant," Bess said, smiling at George. George simply bowed.

Could Señora Ramirez be a terrorist? If so, on which side—the rebels' or the dictator's? Nancy felt a sudden stab of pity for Teresa. She was so alone on her first trip to a foreign country. The man she loved had been brutally murdered, and suddenly she wasn't sure who that man had been. Even her chaperon might betray her.

"Teresa, you stay here. You'll be safe with the guards at the door. Would you like Bess to stay with you?" Nancy asked gently.

Teresa's face was set. "I am coming with you. Perhaps I will remember something more when I am there."

"No one's going *anywhere* till Nancy washes her hair and scrubs that skin dye off," Bess said. "There's a contract out for Teresa Montenegro, remember?"

Nancy and Teresa stared at each other. "Bess is right. You change back. Me, I will be all right as a blond American!" Teresa fairly pushed Nancy toward the shower.

Nancy didn't think it was the time to point out that by then there was probably a contract on her too. She used a few precious minutes to wash the gel out of her hair and to try to scrub away the skin dye. If she looked more deeply tanned than usual, it couldn't hurt much. She pulled on jeans and a shirt.

Then there was a knock on the door. Everybody froze.

"Takeoff time," a detective's voice whispered through the door.

They piled into the car. Nancy was still toweling her wet hair.

During the second wild ride of the night—out to the airport—Teresa sat wrapped in silence, gazing unseeingly at the lights of Washington across the river.

The limousine careened into the airport arrivals area. With Nancy in the lead, George, Bess, Teresa, and their escorts swept toward the novelty store.

The owner was in the shop, and he wasn't in a good mood. "I've been over this twice already with other agents," he snapped. "Why can't you people get your act together? Yes, I was in the shop at the time you mentioned. But I've already said I can't remember every foreigner who walks into this place. Or every native, either!"

"Please!" Nancy forced herself to smile at him. "I know this is annoying, but it's terribly important." She glanced over at Teresa, who was gazing as if hypnotized at the poster for the tennis tournament.

"It's about her—her fiancé!" Nancy told the storekeeper in a low voice. "He's been murdered, and we need to know everything we can about his movements. He bought postcards. He probably bought them here."

"You mean the poor guy I read about in the papers? Is that the girl—Montenero or something—they're talking about?"

He snapped his fingers. "Now I remember! There *was* someone in here buying postcards. I remember him on account of he stared at that poster just the way she's doing. Kind of creepy.

129

And it was weird the way he picked his postcards—just up and down one of the rows, as if the pictures on 'em didn't really matter."

"He was interested in the poster? Did he say anything about the tournament?" Nancy asked urgently.

"Nope. Just stared. And he touched it." The shop owner scratched his head. "That was weird, too, come to think of it. Seemed like it was the poster itself he was interested in, not what it said. I had to tell him to take his big hands off it. We don't let people mess the airport up with graffiti or anything," he added smugly.

Take his hands off the poster . . . Nancy moved toward it as if hypnotized herself. Her eyes swept over it. Then, delicately, her hand reached out to touch one word. *Semi-Pro.*

The dot over the *i* seemed ever so faintly larger than the dot over the *i* in the word *International*, which was set in the same type.

Nancy's index finger touched the dot, her nail scraped against it—and the dot came off in her hand.

She knew what it was even before she heard one of the agents breathe the word behind her shoulder. *"Microdot!"*

Chapter

Sixteen

NANCY KNEW SHE would never forget that frightful night. The stretch limousine must have had a souped-up motor, because the ride away from the airport was a blurred montage of headlights, nightlit monuments, and the Capitol dome glowing like a beacon in the distance.

The federal agent at the wheel did not volunteer where they were headed. Nancy didn't ask. She was well aware that if time hadn't been so urgent, she and her friends wouldn't have been allowed to go along.

Sometime during the evening, a light rain had begun to fall. The dark streets gleamed, and raindrops streaked the windshield. Nancy stole a glance at her watch. Time was running out!

The limousine tore past the White House. A group of demonstrators huddled forlornly with umbrellas and banners on the far side of the street, under the watchful eye of police.

"Protesting the dictatorship in my country," Teresa said emotionlessly. Her hands were clasped tightly, her face like stone.

At last the limo turned into the entrance to a garage. An armed guard at the entry booth checked the driver's ID. They parked in a cavernous, almost empty enclosure that was brightly lit. Their footsteps echoed as they walked across the concrete, and Nancy noticed that their escorts held guns in their hands.

The driver punched a coded sequence of numbers into an electronic device beside a heavy steel door. For a moment a tiny beam of red light swept their faces. Then, noiselessly, the door slid open.

Surrounded by their armed guard, Nancy and her friends stepped inside into a bright, hospital-white corridor. The steel door slid shut again, and another door concealed in the opposite wall slid open.

Then they were crowded together into a small, futuristic elevator car, which sped upward.

When they stepped out, Nancy fought back a giggle. Unconsciously she'd been expecting a science-fiction laboratory of some kind. But the room they entered was a cross between a drab office and her high school chemistry lab.

The electronics technicians who were waiting for them, though, were all business. As soon as the federal man produced the tiny *i* dot from the poster, it was whisked beneath a high-powered microscope.

Nancy, Teresa, Bess, and George were ushered into a small office and told to stay there.

"Make yourselves some coffee if you want to. There may be something around here to go with it," the man in the lab jacket added. He went out, shutting the office door behind him.

"None of us has had any dinner yet, come to think of it," George said in a flat voice. "Not that it matters."

Bess tasted the coffee that was left in the glass pot and made a face. "This is awful." She emptied the pot, washed it, refilled it, and turned on the machine. Nancy rummaged in the small cupboard for the "something" the scientist had referred to. Her stomach felt like lead, but she had to keep her hands busy. She found a box of crackers and a jar of cheese spread and began making snacks for everyone.

George paced between the window and the door. Teresa sat on a plaid daybed, looking like a statue.

The coffeepot steamed, sending out the strong, comforting smell of brewing coffee. The clock ticked away. Eleven-thirty. Midnight. One A.M. Two A.M.

"Why don't they tell us something?" Nancy exclaimed at last.

"Remember the old saying, no news is good news." Bess pressed a third mug of coffee into Nancy's hand.

Nancy set it down so hard that the scalding liquid splashed her wrist. "I can't stand this. I have to know!"

She opened the office door. At once a young woman in a lab coat appeared. "I'm sorry. It's really much better if you stay in there."

"Tell me something!" Nancy pleaded.

"You were right. It *was* a microdot—a piece of film. The list is on it. We still haven't been able to crack the code, but all the mechanics of protection have been set up. Agents in all the major cities of the U.S. are standing ready to provide protection for the people on that list as soon as the names are decoded. And now I must get back to my computer!"

She vanished again.

"A lot of good protection will do if it comes too late," George muttered as Nancy made her report.

Teresa's eyes were closed, and her lips moved silently.

Three A.M. Four.

Bess had fallen asleep. Even George was

drowsing. Nancy struggled against the heaviness in her eyelids.

She thought she was awake, but all the same the faint creak as the office door opened made her jump. Dan stood silhouetted in the doorway, his face one broad grin.

"It's okay. They've cracked the code. The FBI has gone to everybody's rescue." Dan went over and kissed Bess awake. "Come on, honey. I'm taking you girls home."

As they headed for the elevator an older man came toward them. He was dressed in an immaculate navy-blue suit, but his tie was askew. "Which one of you is Nancy Drew?" he asked.

Nancy stepped forward, and he shook her hand firmly. "A fine job. Senator Kilpatrick said you were good, and she was right. Thanks to you, a lot of people are going to sleep better from now on."

"Has El Morro been caught?" Nancy asked at once.

"You'll be hearing all about it in the morning. I understand the senator's planning a news conference." The agent smiled warmly and went back to his office.

The limousine repeated its ride through the Washington streets. "Stop a minute," Dan ordered as it passed an all-night fast-food restaurant. He went in and returned with bags of hamburgers, french fries, and sodas.

When they reached the hotel, they carried them up to their suite. Dan intended to sleep on the sitting-room sofa again, and Teresa would have the other bed in Nancy's room. Her chaperon was still being detained for questioning.

By the time they finished eating, the first streaks of light were in the eastern sky.

"I can't go to sleep now! Can you find out—have all the people on the list been warned in time?" Nancy asked Dan.

Dan telephoned Senator Kilpatrick's office and in a few minutes turned back to Nancy jubilantly.

"It's okay! We got to 'em in time! So far El Morro's escaped capture, but there's a dragnet out for him. At eight o'clock this morning the senator's going to go on the air to announce that San Carlos's president-for-life has fled his palace. The revolution is underway, but Senator Kilpatrick has been able to help those political leaders she's been meeting with work out a coalition government."

"So there's no reason for El Morro to hang around here, especially if he's just a hired assassin," George commented.

"Right. There are a lot of people watching for him at the airports. He'll probably head for home, wherever that is, as soon as the senator announces that all five people on the hit list are now under U.S. government protection. Then we'll nab him."

Nancy jerked upright. "*Five* people?"

"Sure." Dan rattled them off.

"But there were supposed to be six! Roberto told Senator Kilpatrick there were six!"

"You probably just heard wrong," Dan said kindly.

"We didn't! Dan, I beg you, call the lab! Ask if a name could have been taken off the list!" Dan shook his head, but he picked up the phone anyway.

When he turned back to Nancy, his face had changed. "You were right. There are indications that something was deleted. Probably some kind of accident when the dot was brought through a radar check. They're putting a crew to work again right now."

Already the gray in the sky was growing paler. Nancy looked at her watch. There wasn't enough time!

What could the sixth name on the list have been? Suppose it hadn't been taken off by accident or by mistake?

Who was the most prominent person in the United States working for the peaceful overthrow of the San Carlos dictator?

The realization struck Nancy like a blow. Senator Marilyn Kilpatrick—the person Roberto had been trying to smuggle information to! Senator Kilpatrick, who in a few more hours would be announcing the dictator's flight and the transition of power!

Roberto must have been planning to let Senator Kilpatrick be murdered. Maybe he figured that with her out of the way there'd be no one to finger him. Certainly his San Carlos associates would have killed him if they discovered he'd sold out.

It was the only thing Nancy could come up with to explain the missing name. But the main thing was to save the senator. What Roberto had brought to the U.S. was a *photo* of the hit list. The killer had the *original* list—and the senator's name was still on it!

"We've got to warn the senator!" Nancy shouted to Dan. "She's the sixth person, I'm sure of it. Call her, quick!"

Dan's jaw dropped. "I don't know where she is! Nobody seems to. She doesn't think she's in any danger, so she slipped her guards and went out for an early breakfast somewhere with your father."

Chapter

Seventeen

THE WORLD SEEMED to turn upside down in front of Nancy's eyes. Then it righted itself. Just as at that moment on the tennis court, she saw the danger and knew the only thing to do.

"George! Call the senator's office. Tell them she's on the hit list. Dan, come on!" Nancy dashed for the door.

George was already on the phone.

"Where are we going?" Dan demanded as he and Nancy ran down the corridor.

"To find my dad. I know the places he likes to eat in D.C." Not waiting for the elevator, Nancy lunged for the emergency stairs and went down them two at a time.

Dan reached his car and unlocked the doors. "I'm driving," Nancy announced. "You get on the phone with the feds," she ordered Dan.

Dan tossed over the keys and jumped into the passenger seat. The phone beeped as Nancy jerked the car out of its parking space and catapulted it up the runway.

She was barely conscious of Dan's voice speaking tersely into the phone receiver. Nancy's eyes were on the road, which was already gilded with sunlight. Her mind clicked along like a computer.

She knew that Senator Kilpatrick had scheduled an eight o'clock video press conference in her office. That meant Carson Drew must have taken her to eat somewhere nearby. Someplace he liked near the Capitol and the Senate Office Building. Someplace he knew would be very quiet and private.

"Tell the feds to check the Monocle! And the American Café!" Nancy shouted.

She floored the gas pedal as she roared north on Washington Street. Horns honked. Somewhere behind them a siren sounded.

Dan broke his phone connection and beeped his own police station. He identified himself and his car license number crisply. "Requesting black-and-white on our tail. Repeat, request escort immediately." Dan gave a code number that Nancy guessed meant urgent security business.

Almost at once the police car fell into place behind them, its siren magically clearing the way in front. "Heading into D.C.," Dan said into the telephone as Nancy shot onto the road leading to the Arlington Memorial Bridge. And then, "Where to?"

"I don't know." All Nancy knew was that *something* was driving *her,* as if the car and her subconscious had one common will. "The Watergate, I guess. Just in case. It's closest—"

Golden sun sparkled on the Potomac and on the white marble of the statues as they tore across the bridge. The Kennedy Center for the Performing Arts shimmered peacefully in the sunlight. The curved lines of the Watergate's many balconies glistened.

They careened to a stop at the hotel entrance, and Dan leaned out. "Seen Senator Kilpatrick this morning?" he called to a uniformed doorman.

"Negative. Nobody important stirring around here yet. I just checked." The doorman indicated a tiny radio concealed in his hand.

Dan waved to him and pulled his head in again. "Government security, undercover, on account of the San Carlos crowd in town," he told Nancy.

The phone beeped. Dan flipped the loudspeaker button, so the voice echoed tinnily through the car. "Negative on American Café and Monocle. Lady's own guards can't find her.

141

She pulled a cute stunt and shook them. Don't know who she's with, but they must have wanted to be real private."

Privacy was one thing, but Nancy had a feeling El Morro was not as easy to elude as the senator's own security people.

Suddenly Nancy let out a cry. Her right hand found the emergency brake and jerked it free as her right foot slammed down again on the gas pedal.

The car leaped forward.

"Where?" Dan yelled.

"The Hay-Adams Hotel! Dad was there last trip—the first time he'd seen it since it was restored. He said something about how beautiful it was, and convenient—and what a good place to have a conference, because you couldn't be overheard by other tables—"

"Got that?" Dan shouted into the phone. "Left at the next corner, then right at the next light," he ordered Nancy.

Nancy followed his instructions. Out of nowhere, another police car appeared and fell in before them, clearing their way. Nancy's hands were frozen on the steering wheel. She took the right turn on two tires.

They raced through central Washington. The historic Hay-Adams Hotel loomed ahead of them. Nancy screeched to a stop, burning rubber against the curb.

As fast as Dan and the other police were

getting out of their cars, Nancy was faster. She raced across the sidewalk, almost knocking down two people who were in her way. Then she ran through the entrance doors, through the lobby, and past a sign directing patrons to a breakfast buffet. Nancy's lungs burned as she exploded into the high-ceilinged serenity of the Victorian restaurant.

Her eyes swept the room. Suddenly she thought her heart would burst with gratitude. There was Senator Kilpatrick, in a pale gray suit, reaching for her attaché case as Carson Drew rose to pull out her chair.

Something dazzled, the way something had dazzled at the tennis court—

Nancy did not risk the split-second to look for the location of the gun barrel.

"Dad! Get down!" she screamed.

Chapter

Eighteen

COMMUNICATION BETWEEN THE Drews was as good as always. Instantly Carson Drew threw himself forward, directly against Senator Kilpatrick. He knocked her to the ground and rolled with her beneath the table just as the shots rang out.

The bullets hit the crystal goblets on the table. They gave a high musical ping as they shattered.

Somebody screamed.

Within seconds police were everywhere. But the room was shadowy. As police raced in the direction from which the shots had come, Nancy saw a dark figure leap away.

"Dan!" Nancy grabbed his arm.

As Dan swung around, the figure came running straight toward Nancy. The gun was still in his hand. Suddenly, it swung down toward her.

On a table beside Nancy was a vase of red roses. Almost of its own volition, Nancy's hand snatched up the vase and flung it into the assassin's face.

The gun fired upward, exploding crystal drops of a chandelier. At the same moment, Dan leaped forward in a flying tackle.

Soon four burly policemen were cuffing the assassin and reading him his rights. The crimson splotches on the carpet were rose petals, not blood.

Nancy ran into her father's arms.

That night, a jubilant party gathered in Senator Kilpatrick's box to watch Teresa Montenegro's triumphant victory in the International Semi-Pro Women's Tennis Tournament. They had kept their excitement under control during the earlier part of the day, in deference to Teresa's feelings. But now, with Teresa on the court playing her heart out, it could break free.

"At least I arrived in time for the celebrating," Ned Nickerson said, hugging Nancy as Teresa prepared for her last game. "I wish I could have helped you out earlier."

"It helps having you here right now," Nancy said happily. "I'm so glad you came. It's not just anyone who would fly all the way to D.C. just for a tennis match.''

Ned had phoned as soon as Senator Kilpatrick's delayed press conference had gone off the air. The senator, visibly shaken but resolute, had told the world the full story of how Nancy Drew had saved her life at the Hay-Adams Hotel. She had also announced that thanks to Nancy's quick thinking and the fine cooperation of various federal and local law-enforcement agencies, the notorious hired killer, El Morro, had been arrested.

Several lesser terrorists had also been caught up in the federal agents' sweep of various American cities. The U.S. government and the vast majority of people in San Carlos were jubilant. The San Carlos dictator had fled to someplace unknown in South America.

Bess, snuggling in Dan's arms, caught Nancy's eye and giggled. "Everything's working out well for everybody," she said contentedly. "Did you hear that Dan's leaving the police and taking a permanent job on Senator Kilpatrick's staff? He'll *have* to spend a lot of time back in our home state now!"

"We've heard about it three times in the past hour," George said, grinning.

"Even Señora Ramirez has gotten what she deserved," Bess continued happily. Teresa's chaperon was being extradited to San Carlos, where the new provisional government would investigate her strong ties to the former dictator.

"But not everything has worked out," Nancy added, her face growing sober. Involuntarily her eyes went toward the tennis court. As far as the cheering crowd knew, Teresa Montenegro, about to win the tournament with one of her sizzling backhand returns, was on top of the world. But there were so many things the crowd didn't know.

"I should have suspected something," Teresa said to Nancy quietly when they were finally alone together in the locker room. "There was always a part of Roberto that was unreachable. A side of him I didn't understand. I told myself it was because I was still so young. Now I see that he wanted to protect me by not letting me know too much."

She glanced at Nancy, then away. "He *must* have been committed to the revolution, you know. That was why he did what he did. He must have thought that if an American senator was assassinated by orders of the dictator, then the U.S. government would *have* to come in on the rebels' side."

Nancy didn't answer. She was afraid Roberto's reasons had not been so noble. There had been large amounts of money found among his things at the hotel. That was one of the things Senator Kilpatrick had not announced and Teresa didn't know about. Apparently Roberto really had been acting as a double agent. It still wasn't clear whether he had been murdered on orders of the dictator or of the rebels.

"But he did protect you," Nancy said gently.

"Yes, and so did you," Teresa replied gravely. "I hope we shall be friends for a long time."

That was another thing Senator Kilpatrick had not yet announced. Thanks to fast action by her, with help from Carson Drew, Teresa had been granted asylum in the United States.

George came into the locker room. "Hey, you guys, haven't you gotten your stories straight yet? The press is waiting, and so's the senator."

"Coming." Teresa gave her hair a quick shake into place and went out to meet her public, her head high.

Appropriately, Teresa's press conference was held at a table in the Hollins Gymnasium, right under an American flag. Almost immediately, a reporter asked Teresa what her plans were, since civil war had broken out in her country.

Teresa glanced at Senator Kilpatrick, who stepped to the microphone. "I'm happy to announce that Teresa Montenegro has requested and been granted U.S. asylum. She will enter professional tennis in a few months—as an American player! America can be very proud to have her."

"What about your San Carlos coach who was

murdered?" a reporter shouted. "He was more than just your coach, wasn't he?"

Everyone around Teresa stiffened. But Teresa's head was high. "He was my good friend. I am . . . honored . . . to have had him as my coach, my friend. And to have these new friends who are here with me."

Her eyes traveled around the circle—the senator, Carson Drew, Dan and Bess, George. Last of all, Nancy, whose hand was linked with Ned's. Their eyes met. Nancy knew that Teresa's mind, like hers, was whirling back over the terror-filled events of the past few days.

"I am very lucky just to be alive," Teresa said simply. "And that is due most of all to my friend, the—what do you call it? Superstar? The superstar detective, Nancy Drew!"

Nancy's next case:

When Nancy is asked to investigate some terrifying threats to the Emerson College basketball team, she jumps at the chance. After all, Ned is co-captain of the team, so the case will bring them closer together.

Or will it?

Nancy thinks Ned's best friend is the culprit, but Ned can't believe it. He refuses to have anything to do with the case—*or* with Nancy.

Before Nancy has time to work things out, the threats start coming her way. Now she's in danger of losing Ned—*and* her life! Will Nancy win or lose? Find out in *TWO POINTS TO MURDER*, Case #8 in The Nancy Drew Files.

The Nancy Drew Files

by Carolyn Keene

Don't miss these new titles in the Nancy Drew Files, coming in Armada in 1989:

ARMADA

THE CLASS OF '88 SERIES
LINDA A. COONEY

1	HIGH HOPES	£1.95	☐
2	CHANGING IMPRESSIONS	£1.95	☐
3	BREAKING FREE	£1.95	☐
4	REVISED DREAMS	£1.95	☐

For five friends, four years of high school can see a lot of changes.

Well observed stories about five teenagers, Nick, Sean, Celia, Allie and Meg, coping with the excitement and problems of growing up in an American high school.

To order direct from the publishers just tick the titles you want and send your name and address with a cheque/postal order for the price of the book plus postage to:

> Collins Childrens Cash Sales
> PO Box 11
> Falmouth
> Cornwall
> TR10 9EP

Postage: 60p for the first book, 25p for the second book, plus 15p per copy thereafter, to a maximum of £1.90.

ARMADA

EUNICE GOTTLIEB
TRICIA SPRINGSTUBB

This hilarious new series features the irresistible Eunice Gottlieb who spends her time dreaming of breaking away from the chaos of her family. Contemporary, fast-paced and very incisive, these adventures make compulsive reading.

LIFE'S ONE BIG HURDLE   £1.95 ☐

WHICH WAY TO THE NEAREST
  WILDERNESS?   £1.95 ☐

WHY CAN'T LIFE BE A PIECE
   OF CAKE?   £1.95 ☐

To order direct from the publishers just tick the titles you want and send your name and address with a cheque/postal order for the price of the book plus postage to:

> Collins Childrens Cash Sales
> PO Box 11
> Falmouth
> Cornwall
> TR10 9EP

Postage: 60p for the first book, 25p for the second book, plus 15p per copy thereafter, to a maximum of £1.90.

ARMADA

STEVIE DAY SUPERSLEUTH
(that's me!)

I'm on my way to being the first female Commissioner of the Metropolitan Police. It's true I have a few personal problems: for a start I'm small and skinny and people are always mistaking me for a boy. I'm 14 – though you wouldn't think so – and my younger sister, Carla, not only looks older than me but she's much prettier too. Not that that really matters. You see, she doesn't have my brains.

If you want to see my razor-sharp mind in action or have proof of my brilliant powers of deduction then read about my triumphant successes in:

STEVIE DAY: Supersleuth
STEVIE DAY: Lonely Hearts
STEVIE DAY: Rat Race
STEVIE DAY: Vampire

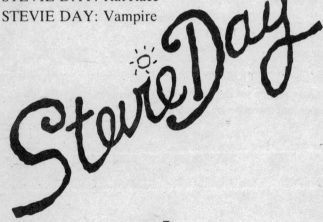

ARMADA